1. The reports went missing in 2012 and nobody __has been__ them since.

(A) sees   (B) saw
(C) has seen   (D) was seen

went missing 視了
= was lost
= disappeared

命令句可表「條件」，and 表「背」，
or 表「否定」。

lab n. 實驗室 (= laboratory)

3. Henry was away from home for quite a bit and __seldom__ saw his family.

(A) frequently   (B) seldom
(C) always   (D) usually

was away from home 在家
= was not home

nothing much 沒什麼
= nothing important
= nothing special
= nothing worth mentioning
  沒什麼值得提的

5. There are still many problems __to be solved__ [before we are ready for a long stay on the moon]

(A) solving   (B) solved
(C) being solved   (D) __to be solved__

since 是 冬冬ㄐ...連用，在此，
since

He c

si
a

2. __Call__ me tomorrow.
   B
you know the lab result.

(A) Calling   (B) Call
(C) To call   (D) Having called

= If you call me tomorrow, I'll let you know …

not at home (暫時) 不在家
quite a bit 很多時間
= quite a bit of time
= quite a lot

4. — What did you do last
   A   weekend?
   — Oh, nothing __much__.

(A) much   (B) else
(C) ever   (D) yet

many problems to be solved
不定詞表「未平」，分詞暗示「已有的
經驗。

6. [__Even though__ (Although) (那麼) the forest park
   C is far away,] a lot of tourists visit it every year.

(A) As   (B) When
(C) __Even though__
(D) In case

7. The best moment for the football
B   star was __when__ he scored
    the winning goal.
    名詞子句

    (A) where   (B) when
    (c) how   (D) why

    goal n. 目標; 得分進球
    score the winning goal
    踢進致勝的一球

8. The book has helped me greatly
D   in my daily communication,

    (A) in place   (B) in order
        在適當的位置   有秩序

    (c) in shape   (D) in fashion
                          流行

    ⎰ go jogging 去慢跑
    ⎱ = go for a jog
      run slowly 跑得慢(字力不行)
      push-up n. 伏地挺身
    ⎰ stay in shape 保持健康
    ⎱ = stay healthy

11. The lecture __having been given__,
D   a lively question-and-answer
        熱烈的   問   答
    session followed.
       時間
    (A) was given   (B) having given
    (c) to be given
    (D) having been given

    演講結束後, 接著是熱烈的問答
    時間。
    = After the lecture had been
    given,

especially at work, __where__
good impression is a must.
                        必備之物
(A) which   (B) when
(c) as   (D) where

at work ① 在工作吧是
        ② 在工作時

9. Tom always goes jogging in
C   the morning, and he usuall
    does push-ups to stay in sha

10. I can't meet you on Sunda
D   I'll be __otherwise__ occupie
    (A) also   (B) just
    (c) nevertheless (D) otherwise

    I'll be otherwise occupied.
    我有別的事要忙。
    = I'll be busy in other respect
    otherwise adv. ①否則 ②在其他方面
    occupy v. ①佔據 ②使忙碌

副子 → 分構
①去連 ②去掉同主詞 ③ V→ V-ing

12. — __Dear me__! Somebody ha
A   left the lab door open.
    — Don't look at me.

    (A) Dear me   (B) Hi, there
                       = Hi

    (c) Thank goodness
        = Thank God 感謝上帝

    (D) Come on 快點

Dear me! 天哪阿!
= My God!
= My Goodness!
= Oh, my goodness!
= Goodness!
= Heavens!

13. The exact year _which_ Angela and her family spent together vt. in China was 2008.
(A) when (B) where (C) why (D) which

which 有代名作用, when 無。

14. The twins, who _had finished_ their homework, were allowed to play badminton on the playground.
羽毛球   球場
(A) will finish   (B) finish
(C) have finished
(D) had finished

過去的過去, 用「過去完成式」。

15. You can ask anyone for help. _Everyone_ here is willing to lend you a hand.
(A) One   (B) No one
(C) Everyone   (D) Someone

lend sb. a hand
幫助某人
= give sb. a hand
= help sb.

16. The meaning of the word "nice" changed a few times _before_ it finally came to include the sense "pleasant".
意義
(A) before   (B) after
(C) since   (D) while

What a nice day!
   pleasant
You are so nice!
   kind
依句意選(A) before 。

17. Terry, please _look up from_ your cell phone when Grandma is talking to you.
(A) look up from
(B) look into 調查
(C) look back on 回顧
(D) look through 匆匆…看
look up 往上看

18. When the sports hero _turned up_ at our party, he was welcomed 熱烈歡迎 with open arms.
(A) turned up
   出現
(B) left off
   停止
(C) moved on
   繼續前進
(D) got away
   離開

turn up 出現
= show up
= appear

19. B
[while waiting for the opportunity to get _promoted_] Henry did his best to perform his duty.

(A) promote   (B) promoted
(C) promoting   (D) to promote

{ get promoted 得到晉升
{ perform one's duty 盡職
   = do one's duty

20. C
It's our hope [that we will play a greater role in the marketplace and, _therefore_ 因此 supply more jobs.]
market

(A) however   (B) anywhere
(C) therefore   (D) otherwise

{ play a role 扮演一個角色
{ = play a part

21. B
Shakespeare's writing is still 寫作 popular today. It has really _stood_ the test of time.

(A) failed   (B) stood
(C) taken   (D) conducted

stand the test of time
經得起時間的考驗 (可用 pass)

22. C
They chose Tom to be _the_ captain of the team [because they knew he was _a_ smart leader.]

(A) a; the   (B) the; the
(C) the; a   (D) a; a

the captain of the team
隊長 [指定]
a smart leader 一個聰明的 領導者 [不指定]

23. C
Thanks for your directions to the house; we wouldn't have found it _otherwise_.

(A) nowhere   (B) however
(C) otherwise   (D) instead
否則 (副詞作連接詞)
[文法 p.474]

24. D
Starting your own business 動名詞 would be a way to achieve financial independence. _On the other hand_, it could just put you in debt.
使你負債

(A) In other words 換句話說
(B) All in all 總之
(C) As a result 因此
(D) On the other hand

{ on the other hand 另一方面; 然而
{ = however
{ = nevertheless
{ = nonetheless
{ = yet

如何學英文文法？

　　爲了學文法，40多年前我聽遍全台灣補習班老師的課，最後在嘉義道成補習班，聽到班主任王伯怡老師的文法課，他很瘦，不到40公斤，他說的中文和英文都聽不太懂，但是板書很整齊。他發明句子分析法，找出英文句子的主詞和動詞，我整整聽了一年，沒有一次缺課，學會了他的方法，在台南一中對面的百達天主教堂開課，由我弟弟找了8位台南一中的同學，開始上課，現在台大醫學系的名教授王主科醫師，就是我當年的學生，我很感謝王伯怡老師和當時補習班的員工。

　　我對文法瘋狂，40年前就開始教文法，把講義編成「文法寶典」，文法是語言的歸納，規則無限多，例外也無限多，一輩子也教不完，也學不完。後來發覺口語很重要，請了一位美籍老師 Edward McGuire，隨身陪著我練習英語，每天我們在一起，我拿著錄音機和他講話，晚上再把錄音機錄起來的話，寫下來修正，還是沒有用。有一年我下了狠工夫，把補習班交給別人經營，和外國老師到美國待了三個月，每天看英文小說，不懂就問他，好的句子劃出來背，效果還是有限，因爲學了會忘記。有一次，和外國人在夏威夷海灘，聽到他說：It's not too hot. It's not too cold. It's just right. 我突然發現，以三句一組說英文該有多好？於是在2003年，發明了「一口氣背會話」，以三句爲一組、九句爲一段，從此，不需要外國人陪伴，自己就會說英文了。

　　把「一口氣背會話」用在兒童美語，小孩子學得很快，衍生出「兒童英語話劇」和「兒童英語演講」，但是到了國一，會說話的小孩子，文法題不會寫，不得不向傳統教學法低頭，很多兒童美語補習班，由於不教文法，小孩上國中，考試成績不理想而離開。可見，兒童美語有問題，會說不會寫，傳統教學也有問題，會考試不會說話。英文學了那麼久，見到外國人

卻不會說，是很痛苦的事，少數會說的人，中國人聽不懂，以為他們很厲害，外國人認為他們是中國人，會說就不錯了，事實上，他們心裡虛得很，因為自己沒有信心，不知道說得對不對。有位美國馬里蘭大學的碩士，回到台灣，滿嘴的英文，我請她把她說的話寫下來，給外國老師一改，錯誤百出。

有了「一口氣背會話」，只要背就會說，背的語言說出來最有信心，但是考試呢？經過十幾年的研究，終於發明了「一口氣背文法」，每一句代表一個文法規則，一個單元九句，就學了九個文法規則，這些話有劇情，天天都可以說。我曾經應我的學生任延玲校長的邀請，到廈門瑞爾英語，給他們的老師培訓，有老師問我，兒童學會文法，那單字呢？背完「一口氣背文法」216 句，英文文法有整體的概念後，要不斷地演練文法題，先做升高中的題目，再做大陸升大學的題目，大陸的文法試題，題目出得好，沒有什麼太艱深的單字，如：

Unless some extra money _____, the theater will close.
A. was found   B. finds
C. is found   D. found   【答案C】

這題出自 2014 年，大陸全國統一考試。把試題當做教材，既能增加英文閱讀能力，無形中也增加了單字量。我覺得，學英文最怕目標不明確，東學一點、西學一點，「劉毅英文」教同學背演講，一篇一篇背，有成就感。「一口氣背文法」目標是，背 216 個句子，再做 450 條文法題，相信孩子的文法無人能比。

劉毅

CONTENTS

TEST 1

請依照上下文意，選出一個最正確答案，每題 4 分。

1. On my way to school each day, I generally _____ many dogs and cats.
   A. were seeing   B. am seeing
   C. see   D. was seen   【明治大】

2. Water _____ at a temperature of 100 degrees centigrade.
   A. boils   B. is boiling
   C. was boiling   D. used to boil   【上智大】

3. She _____ to the U.S. three times when she was a college student.
   A. went   B. would go
   C. used to go   D. has gone   【松山大】

4. I have no idea when he _____ again.
   A. come   B. has come
   C. coming   D. will come   【玉川大】

5. I _____ lunch at the moment. Can you come back later?
   A. had   B. have had
   C. am having   D. had had   【松山大】

6. They _____ at Narita tomorrow.

    A. arrived

    B. are arriving

    C. is going to arrive

    D. will be arrived 【東北學院大】

7. When it began to rain, the girls _____ outside.

    A. will play

    B. are playing

    C. were playing

    D. have played 【鹿兒島國際大】

8. I don't think I can meet you at six tomorrow night.

    _____

    A. I'll still be working

    B. I'll still work

    C. I'm still at work

    D. I'm still working 【七試】

9. My brother _____ his company's basketball team.

    A. is belonging

    B. is belonging to

    C. belongs to

    D. belongs 【桃山學院大】

10. The plane leaves at 6:00, and Kevin _____ at the
    airport yet.
    A. doesn't arrive   B. hasn't arrived
    C. won't be arrived   D. isn't arrived   【廣島修道大】

11. I know all about that film because I _____ it twice.
    A. am seeing
    B. have been seeing
    C. will be seeing
    D. have seen   【阪南大】

12. John and Mary _____ each other since 1976.
    A. have been knowing
    B. have known
    C. were knowing
    D. were known   【七試】

13. Tom _____ to San Francisco to see a friend of his
    last month.
    A. goes   B. is going
    C. has gone   D. went   【濱松大】

14. He _____ home just now. Didn't you know that?
    A. comes   B. came
    C. has come   D. had come   【拓殖大】

15. When Bill got to school, the class _____ already.
    A. started   B. was starting
    C. has started   D. had started   【セ試】

16. We _____ for nearly thirty minutes when the train arrived.
    A. had been waiting
    B. have been waiting
    C. have waited
    D. will have waited   【獨協大】

17. I lost the watch which my sister _____ me for my birthday.
    A. gives   B. has given
    C. had given   D. will give   【京都学園大】

18. By next week you _____ the package.
    A. will have received
    B. receiving   C. received
    D. have received   【セ試】

19. When I _____ at the airport, I will call you back.
    A. will arrive   B. arrived
    C. would arrive   D. arrive   【流通経済大】

20. I will wait here until she _____.
    A. came   B. come
    C. comes   D. will come   【北海学園大】

21. You can come and see me anytime if you _____ free tomorrow.

    A. will   B. are

    C. were   D. will be   【中京大】

22. "Is Bill still using your car?" "Yes, I wonder when he _____ it."

    A. has returned   B. returned

    C. returns   D. will return   【七試】

23. I don't know if he _____ back next spring.

    A. will come   B. come

    C. came   D. had come   【流通經濟大】

24. Some books will be forgotten as soon as we _____ them.

    A. have read   B. will have read

    C. will read   D. reading   【流通經濟大】

25. _____ for three hours but we haven't gotten to town yet.

    A. We would walk

    B. We walk

    C. We are walking

    D. We have been walking   【濱松大】

Test 1 詳解

1. **C** *On my way to school each day*, I *generally* <u>see</u> many
dogs and cats. 我每天上學途中，我通常<u>看到</u>很多狗和貓。

表示現在的習慣，用「現在式」。

2. **A** Water <u>boils</u> *at a temperature of 100 degrees centigrade.*

水在攝氏 100 度時<u>沸騰</u>。

表示不變的真理，用「現在式」。

degree 作「度數」解，通常是複數形，即使是「零度」，也
說成 zero degrees。

3. **A** She <u>went</u> to the U.S. *three times* **when** *she was a college*

student. 她唸大學時<u>去過</u>美國三次。

凡是過去某一點時間、某一段時間，或過去的經驗，用
「過去式」。從過去到現在的經驗，才用「現在完成式」。

【比較】 She *has been to* the U.S. *many times.*

She *went* to the U.S. *many times last year.*

4. **D** I have no idea **when** he <u>will come</u> again.
我不知道他何時<u>會再來</u>。

I have no idea 相當於 I don't know，後面可接名詞子句，
表未來就用「未來式」。

5. **C** I am having lunch *at the moment*. Can you come back
later? 我現在<u>正在吃午餐</u>。你能不能待會兒再回來？

at the moment 現在（= *now*）

have 當「有」解時，是狀態動詞，沒有進行式，本句中的
have 指「吃」（= *eat*），表示現在正在做，用「現在進行式」。

  I ***am having*** lunch now.

= I ***am eating*** lunch now.

6. **B** They <u>are arriving</u> *at Narita tomorrow*. 他們明天到成田。

Narita〔nəˈritə〕*n.* 成田（機場）

來去動詞可用現在式、現在進行式和未來式，表未來。

這句話等於：They ***arrive*** at Narita tomorrow.【較常用】

                They ***will arrive*** at Narita tomorrow.【較少用】

7. **C** ***When*** *it began to rain*, the girls <u>were playing</u> *outside*.

開始下雨時，女孩們<u>正在外面玩</u>。

表示過去某時正在進行的動作，用「過去進行式」。

8. **A** I don't think I can meet you *at six tomorrow night*.
<u>I'll still be working.</u>

我想明天晚上 6 點鐘，我無法和你碰面。<u>我還在工作</u>。

表示未來某時正在進行的動作，用「未來進行式」。

9. **C**　My brother <u>belongs to</u> his company's basketball team.

我的兄弟<u>屬於</u>他公司的籃球隊。

belong to（屬於）是狀態動詞，無進行式，其他如：have
（有）、live（住）、own（擁有）、need（需要）。【詳見
「文法寶典」p.343】

中國人的觀念中，把哥哥和弟弟分得很清楚，英文中
brother 可指「哥哥」或「弟弟」。

10. **B**　The plane leaves *at 6:00, **and*** Kevin <u>hasn't arrived</u> *at*
the airport yet.

飛機將在 6 點起飛，而凱文<u>還沒到</u>機場。

「現在完成式」常和 just（剛才）、already（已經）、now
（現在）、yet（尚未，要用否定或疑問）等副詞連用。

11. **D**　I know all about that film ***because*** I <u>*have seen*</u> *it twice.*

那部電影我全部都知道，因為我<u>看過</u>兩次。

「現在完成式」和 once（一次）、twice（二次）、often
（常常）、ever（曾經）、never（從來沒有）等連用，表
示從過去到現在的經驗。

12. **B**　John and Mary <u>have known</u> each other *since 1976.*

約翰和瑪麗從 1976 年就<u>認識</u>了。

「現在完成式」和 since（自從）、for（持續）、how long
（多久）連用，表示從過去到現在的持續動作。

13. **D** Tom <u>went</u> to San Francisco *to see a friend of his last month.*

湯姆上個月去舊金山看他一個朋友。

過去的一點時間，如 yesterday，last night，… ago，
用「過去式」。

14. **B** He <u>came</u> home *just now.* Didn't you know that?

他剛剛才到家。你不知道嗎？

just now 指「剛剛；剛才」(= *a very short time ago*) 時，
用過去式；指「此刻；這時」(= *at the present time*) 時，
用現在式，如：He is not at home *just now*. (他此時不
在家。)

15. **D** *When Bill got to school,* the class <u>had started</u> *already.*

當比爾到學校時，課已經開始了。

①過去某時已經完成的動作，用「過去完成式」。
②過去的過去，用「過去完成式」。

16. **A** We <u>had been waiting</u> *for nearly thirty minutes **when the train arrived.***

當火車到達時，我們已經等了將近三十分鐘。

過去某時已經完成，並持續進行的動作，用「過去完成進
行式」。

17. **C** I lost the watch *which* my sister *had given* me for my *birthday*.

我把姐姐在我生日時，送我的錶弄丟了。

過去的過去，用「過去完成式」。

18. **A** *By next week* you will have received the package.

到了下個星期，你就會收到包裹。

未來某時已經完成的動作，用「未來完成式」。

19. **D** *When I arrive at the airport*, I will call you back.

當我到達機場時，我會回你電話。

表「時間」的副詞子句，常用現在式代替未來式，未來的時間在主要子句中表達。

20. **C** I will wait *here until she comes*.

我會在這裡等，直到她來。

until 引導表「時間」的副詞子句，修飾 wait，用現在式代替未來式。

21. **B** You can come and see me anytime *if you are free tomorrow*.

如果你明天有空，你可以隨時來看我。

表「條件」的副詞子句，多用現在式代替未來式。

22. **D** "Is Bill still using your car?" "Yes, I wonder when he <u>will return</u> it."

「比爾是不是還在用你的車子？」「是的，我不知道他何時會歸還。」

when 引導名詞子句，做 wonder 的受詞，名詞子句要用 will 表示未來。

23. **A** I don't know *if he <u>will come back next spring</u>.*
    ‖   名詞子句
   whether

我不知道他明年春天是否會回來。

if 引導名詞子句接在 ask, see, try, wonder, know 等字之後，表懷疑或詢問時，等於 whether。
名詞子句要用 will 表示未來。

24. **A** Some books will be forgotten *as soon as* we <u>have read</u> *them.* 有些書我們一讀完就會忘記。

as soon as 引導表「時間」的副詞子句，不能用 shall, will 表示未來，要用現在式代替未來式，或用現在完成式代替未來完成式。

25. **D** <u>We have been walking</u> *for three hours* **but** we haven't gotten to town *yet.*

我們已經走了三個小時，但是我們尚未到達城裡。

到現在為止已經完成，並在繼續的動作，用「現在完成進行式」。

TEST 2

請依照上下文意，選出一個最正確答案，每題4分。

1. English and French _____ in Canada.
   A. speak
   B. spoke
   C. are spoken
   D. are spoke 　　　　　　　　　【攝南大】

2. The university library _____ for the last ten years.
   A. is closed
   B. closes
   C. has been closed
   D. closed 　　　　　　　　　【高岡法科大】

3. He was _____ as their leader.
   A. looking up
   B. looked up
   C. looking up to
   D. looked up to 　　　　　　　　　【龍谷大】

4. I was made _____ for a long time.
   A. wait
   B. to wait
   C. waiting
   D. waited 　　　　　　　　　【千葉工大】

5. Carl was seen _____ the building last night.
   A. enter
   B. entering
   C. to enter
   D. having entered 　　　　　　　　　【拓殖大】

6. They say that he studied abroad when he was young.

He is said _____ abroad when he was young.

  A. to study

  B. studying

  C. to have studied

  D. having studied 　　　　　　　　　　　　　　【松山大】

7. His leg was broken when he got _____ by the truck.

  A. overrun

  B. run over

  C. driven in

  D. hit on 　　　　　　　　　　　　　　【札幌學院大】

8. I was deeply _____ with myself after losing the race.

  A. disappointed

  B. disappointing

  C. disappoint

  D. disappointment 　　　　　　　　　　　　　　【昭利女子大】

9. He will not _____ such a small salary.

  A. satisfy with

  B. be satisfied with

  C. be satisfied by

  D. satisfy 　　　　　　　　　　　　　　【東北工大】

10. I was so _____ in the book I didn't hear the phone ring.
    A. absorbed
    B. concerned
    C. engaged
    D. surprised 　　　　　　　　　【廣島女學院大】

11. The car broke down, and we _____ a taxi.
    A. must have gotten
    B. had got to get
    C. had to get
    D. must get 　　　　　　　　　　　【慶大】

12. He was a very stubborn person and _____ not listen to me.
    A. would
    B. could
    C. should
    D. might 　　　　　　　　　　【九州國際大】

13. She has not come here yet. I am afraid she _____ her way.
    A. may be lost
    B. may have lost
    C. may be having lost
    D. may have been lost 　　　　　　　　【京都產業大】

14. Can you lend me something _____? I don't have a pen.
    A. to write
    B. to write on
    C. to write with
    D. to write for 　　　　　　　　【神戶松蔭女子學院大】

15. Ken was very foolish _____ out in this storm.
   A. go   B. to going
   C. of going   D. to go   【四天王寺國際仏教大】

16. The child tried hard _____.
   A. not to cry   B. to not cry
   C. to cry not   D. crying not   【大阪學院大】

17. The gentleman insisted on _____ the money.
   A. my receiving
   B. my reception
   C. me to receive
   D. I should receive   【九州産大】

18. I can use a computer, but when it comes _____ them,
   I know nothing.
   A. repair
   B. for repairing
   C. to repairing
   D. being repaired   【東京電機大】

19. We had a lot of difficulty _____ his new house.
   A. to try arriving
   B. trying to find
   C. to try to find
   D. trying to arrive   【青山學院大】

20. This novel is worth _____.
    A. read   B. reading
    C. to read   D. to be read   【中京大】

21. I don't feel _____ waiting any longer.
    A. useful   B. necessary
    C. like   D. after   【早大】

22. Jane can play the violin, not to _____ the guitar.
    A. speak   B. say
    C. talk   D. mention   【聖心女大】

23. She is _____ buy everything.
    A. enough rich to
    B. enough to rich
    C. rich enough to
    D. rich to enough   【國學院大】

24. No one objected _____ the mountain.
    A. climb   B. for climbing
    C. to climb   D. to climbing   【攝南大】

25. I am not at all used to _____ like that.
    A. treated   B. treating
    C. being treated   D. treat   【工學院大】

Test 2 詳解

1. **C** English and French <u>are spoken</u> *in Canada.*
完全不及物動詞片語

在加拿大說英語和法語。

及物動詞，非人當主詞要用被動，及物動詞的被動，是完全不及物動詞片語。

2. **C** The university library <u>has been closed</u> *for the last ten*

years.

這所大學圖書館過去十年來<u>一直沒開放</u>。

因為有 for …，要用現在完成式，非人做主詞應用被動，所以用「現在完成被動式」。

> 【注意】The library is closed. 【正】
> 　　　　The library is *opened.* 【誤】
> 　　　　The library is open. 【正】
>
> 你可以常説：I'm open 24/7. (我任何時間都可以。)
> 　　　　　　I'm never closed. (我從不打烊。)
> 　　　　　　Call me if you have time.
> 　　　　　　(有時間打電話給我。)
>
> 會説這三句話，你就知道 open 和 closed 的區別。

3. **D** He was <u>looked up to</u> *as their leader.*
主詞補語【as 相當於 to be】

他被尊稱為他們的領袖。

這句話主動形式為：They *looked up to* him *as* their leader.

look up to 尊敬【字面意思是「向上看」，後接 as，用法和 think of A as B 相同，指「認為 A 是 B」】

4. **B** I was made <u>to wait</u> *for a long time.* 我被迫等了很久。

這句話主動形式為：Someone *made* me *wait* for a long time. 使役動詞改被動，須用 *to wait*。

5. **B** Carl was seen <u>entering</u> the building *last night.*

卡爾昨晚被看到<u>進入</u>大樓。

> 這句話主動為：Someone *saw* Carl *entering* the building last night.
>
> 感官動詞接受詞後，可接原形或現在分詞做受詞補語，無意中看到或聽到的用現在分詞，特意的用原形動詞。【詳見「文法寶典」p.420】
>
> 【比較】*Carl was seen to enter the building last night.*
>
> > 【誤，因為非特意】
> >
> > Carl was seen entering the building last night.
> >
> > 【正，無意中看到】
> >
> > 感官動詞改被動，現在分詞不變。

6. **C** They say *that* he studied *abroad* *when* he was young.

He is said <u>to have studied</u> *abroad* *when* he was young.

據說，他年輕時在國外<u>讀過書</u>。

They say that he studied... 的被動式有二種：

① It *is* said that he *studied* ….

② He *is* said *to have studied* ….

前後時態相同，用簡單不定詞，前後時態不一致，用「完成式不定詞」，表示比主要動詞先發生。

7. **B** His leg was broken *when he got* run over *by the truck.*

當他被卡車輾過時，他的腿斷了。

run over「輾過」，被動為 be run over by「被…輾過」，be 動詞可用 get 代替，這句話也可說成：…when he was run over by the truck.

8. **A** I was *deeply* disappointed *with myself* after *losing the race.*

比賽輸了，我對自己深感失望。

情感動詞 disappoint（使失望）、interest（使有興趣）、excite（使興奮）等，原則上用過去分詞形容人，沒有被動意思，介詞不用 by。

背下面三句，就知道情感動詞的用法：

　The news *disappointed* me.（這個消息使我失望。）

= I was *disappointed* with the news.（我對這個消息失望。）

= The news was *disappointing* to me.（這個消息令我失望。）

【比較】 I am disappointed
{
with the news.【第二常用】
at the news.【最常用】
about the news.【第三常用】
}

9. **B** He will not <u>be satisfied with</u> such a small salary.

他不會<u>滿意</u>這麼少的薪水。

a small salary 很少的薪水（= *a low salary*）

a large salary 很高的薪水（= *a high salary*）

satisfy（使滿意）是情感動詞，be satisfied with 指
「對～滿意」。

10. **A** I was *so* <u>absorbed</u> *in the book I didn't hear the phone ring.*

我太<u>專心</u>看書了，沒聽到電話鈴響。

  be absorbed in 專心於

  $\begin{cases} = \text{be immersed in} \\ = \text{be engrossed in} \\ = \text{be lost in} \end{cases}$

be engaged in 忙於；從事於

【美籍老師說這個答案也可能，但 (A) 最好】

so…that「如此…以致於」，so 後句子短時，that 可省略，
或用逗點（,）代替。

11. **C** The car broke down, ***and*** we <u>had to get</u> a taxi.

車子故障了，我們<u>必須搭</u>計程車。

and 連接二個過去式動詞，表示過去連續二個動作，have
to + 原 V. 表示「必須」，過去式為 had to + 原 V.。
have got to = have to，只能用在現在式，如：I have got
to go. 但是，過去式不能用 had got to，通常只用 had to，
故 (B) 錯。

12. **A** He was a *very* stubborn person ***and*** <u>would</u> not listen
to me.　他非常頑固，不會聽我的。

would 表示過去的習慣。

13. **B** She has not come here *yet*.　I am afraid she <u>may have</u>
<u>lost</u> her way.

她還沒有來。我怕她<u>可能</u>迷路了。

may have p.p. 表示現在推測過去。

14. **C** Can you lend me something <u>*to write with*</u>?　I don't
have a pen.

你能不能借我可以寫字的東西？我沒有筆。

不定詞片語當形容詞用，修飾 something，被它修飾的
something，就是它意義上的受詞，不能再接文法上的受
詞，所以不能寫成 … *something to write with it* (誤)。

15. **D** Ken was very foolish <u>*to go* out *in this storm*</u>.

肯非常愚蠢，這種暴風雨還<u>出去</u>。

不定詞片語當副詞用，修飾形容詞 foolish。

16. **A** The child tried hard <u>*not to cry*</u>.

這個孩子努力忍住<u>不哭</u>。

not 要放在不定詞前，表否定。

17. **A** The gentleman insisted on <u>my receiving the money</u>.

　　　　　　　　　　　　　　　　　　　　　　　　受　詞

這位先生堅持<u>我收下錢</u>。

insist on「堅持」，my receiving the money 作 on 的受詞，動名詞意義上的主詞要用所有格形式，但在此 *my* receiving… 可改成 *me* receiving....。【詳見「文法寶典」p.426】

18. **C** I can use a computer, ***but when*** it comes *to repairing them*, I know nothing.

我會用電腦，但<u>一提到</u>修電腦，我一無所知。

when it comes to + V-ing 一提到…

19. **B** We had a lot of difficulty *trying to find* his new house.

我們<u>試著找到</u>他的新家非常困難。

have difficulty
have trouble ⎬ (*in*) + *V-ing* 做…有困難
have a hard time

have 當「有」解時，後面接情感名詞，接動名詞，在現代英文中，in 常省略。

【比較】 *I have difficulty in speaking English.* 【誤】
　　　　 I have difficulty speaking English. 【正】

20. **B** This novel is worth <u>reading</u>. 這本小說值得<u>讀</u>。

worth「值得的」，是形容詞轉變為介系詞，後面接動名詞有三個條件：①及物動詞②無受詞③用主動。

21. **C**　I don't feel <u>like</u> waiting *any longer.*

我不<u>想</u>再等了。

feel like + V-ing　想要

22. **D**　Jane can play the violin, *not to <u>mention</u> the guitar.*

珍會拉小提琴，更別<u>提</u>吉他了。

> ***not to mention***　更別提【都是獨立不定詞用法】
> = ***not to speak of***
> = ***to say nothing of***
> = let alone
>
> 所謂「獨立不定詞片語」，就是和其他部分沒有文法關聯，獨立存在，也可說是副詞片語，修飾全句，常見的還有：
>
> ***to tell the truth***　老實說；坦白說
> = to speak the truth
> = to say the truth
>
> = to speak frankly
> = to speak sincerely
>
> ***to make a long story short***　簡單地說
> = to cut a long story short
> = to make the story short
>
> = to sum up
> = to be short
>
> 【詳見「文法寶典」p.417】

23. **C** She is <u>rich *enough to* buy everything</u>.

她很<u>有錢</u>，<u>足夠</u>買所有東西。

enough 當副詞，要放在所修飾的形容詞或副詞後，後面接不定詞，enough to 的 to 表「肯定的結果」，too~to + V. 中的 to 表「否定的結果」。

24. **D** No one objected <u>to climbing</u> the mountain.

沒有人反對<u>去登</u>那座山。

$$\left\{ \begin{array}{l} \textbf{\textit{object to}} \ \ 反對 \\ = \textbf{\textit{have an objection to}} \end{array} \right.$$

$$\left\{ \begin{array}{l} = \textbf{\textit{oppose}} \\ = \textbf{\textit{be opposed to}} \end{array} \right.$$

【to 是介系詞，後接動名詞】

25. **C** I *am not at all* **used to** <u>being treated</u> *like that*.

我一點都不習慣<u>被</u>那樣<u>對待</u>。

$$\left\{ \begin{array}{l} \textbf{\textit{be used to}} \ \ 習慣於【to 是介系詞，後接動名詞，依句意用被動】\\ = \textbf{\textit{get used to}} \\ = \textbf{\textit{be accustomed to}} \end{array} \right.$$

TEST 3

請依照上下文意，選出一個最正確答案，每題 4 分。

1. The commuter trains are filled with people ＿＿＿＿＿
   newspapers, books, and magazines.
   A. who reads   B. and read
   C. to read   D. reading   【同志社女子大】

2. I'd like to read books ＿＿＿＿ in easy English.
   A. written   B. wrote
   C. write   D. writing   【高千穗大】

3. All things ＿＿＿＿, I think this is the safest policy.
   A. to consider   B. considering
   C. considered   D. are considered 【愛知工大】

4. He lay on the sofa with his ＿＿＿＿ and soon fell
   asleep.
   A. arms folded   B. arms folding
   C. fold arms   D. folding arms   【七試】

5. ＿＿＿＿ from this angle, the doll looks more attractive.
   A. On viewing   B. To view
   C. Viewed   D. Viewing   【青山學院大】

6. It is time you _____ to study.
   A. begin   B. began
   C. will begin   D. had begun   【東洋大】

7. If I _____ at the station five minutes earlier, I
   could have caught the train.
   A. arrived
   B. had arrived
   C. have arrived
   D. have been arriving   【南山大】

8. If I had worked harder in my twenties, I _____ much
   richer now.
   A. am   B. would be
   C. will be
   D. would have been   【大東文化大】

9. Married men sometimes wish they _____ single.
   A. are   B. were
   C. have been   D. may be   【鹿兒島經大】

10. I would have been completely in despair _____ for
    the help of my friends.
    A. despite   B. if it isn't
    C. if it hadn't been
    D. without   【學習院大】

11. _____ anything happen, please let us know immediately.
    A. If   B. Should
    C. May   D. Since   【拓殖大】

12. It is essential that you _____ there today.
    A. is
    B. are
    C. be
    D. wouldn't   【櫻美林大】

13. I have a friend _____ father runs a very nice restaurant in this town.
    A. his   B. that
    C. who   D. whose   【金澤工大】

14. _____ last night wasn't very comfortable.
    A. The bed I slept
    B. The bed in that I slept
    C. The bed I slept in
    D. The bed in I slept   【慶大】

15. _____ you should have done is call the police.
    A. That   B. Who
    C. Why   D. What   【九州産業大】

16. Reading is to the mind _____ exercise is to the body.

    A. when

    B. that

    C. what

    D. whose 【駒澤大】

17. It was getting dark, and _____ was worse, we couldn't find our hotel.

    A. which   B. that

    C. what   D. but 【立命館大】

18. I met a man _____ I thought was an actor.

    A. which   B. what

    C. who   D. whose 【大阪產業大】

19. If _____ I could speak English as fluently as you!

    A. not   B. so

    C. be   D. only 【南山大】

20. _____ his money, John was not able to pay for lunch.

    A. Have lost

    B. Having lost

    C. He lost

    D. Lost 【南山大】

21. _____ Sunday, the bank was closed.

   A. Being   B. Being it

   C. It being   D. It was   【北海學園大】

22. There are still thirty boys _____ in the room.

   A. waiting

   B. to be waited

   C. to wait

   D. waited   【札幌大】

23. She sat _____ her children.

   A. surround

   B. surrounding

   C. surrounded by

   D. to surround   【西南學院大】

24. I didn't buy anything because I didn't see _____
I wanted.

   A. who   B. whose

   C. which   D. what   【別府大】

25. It doesn't matter _____ she admits her guilt or not.

   A. which   B. that

   C. whether   D. what   【高岡法科大】

Test 3 詳解

1. **D** The commuter trains are filled with people *reading*
   newspapers, books, and magazines.
   通勤火車上擠滿<u>正在看</u>報紙、書和雜誌的人。

   …people *reading*…源自…people *who are reading*…。
   A. → who read。

2. **A** I'd like to read books *written in easy English.*

   我喜歡讀用容易的英文<u>寫</u>的書。

   …books *written*…源自…books *which are written*…。
   形容詞子句 → 分詞片語
   ①去關代②去 be

3. **C** *All things considered*, I think this is the safest policy.
   <u>考慮</u>所有事情後，我認爲這是最安全的政策。

   All things *considered*, …源自 *After* all things *are*
   considered, …。
   副詞子句 → 分詞構句
   ①去連接詞②前後主詞不相同，保留③ are → being，可省略

4. **A** He lay on the sofa *with his arms folded and soon* fell
   asleep. 他躺在沙發上，<u>雙臂交疊</u>，很快就睡著了。

> | with ⎫
without ⎭ + 受詞 + 分詞 | 表伴隨主要動詞的情況，受詞
是人，用現在分詞，受詞是非
人，用過去分詞，arms 是非 |

人，後面接 folded。

lie「躺」的三態爲：lie-lay-lain。

lay「生 (蛋)」的三態爲：lay-laid-laid，可看成半規則動

詞，和 say-said-said 變化相同。

5. **C** *Viewed from this angle*, the doll looks more attractive.

從這個角度看，這個娃娃看起來更動人。

Viewed from…源自 *If the doll is viewed* from…。

view 這個字主要當名詞用，作「觀點；視力；景觀」解，

在此當動詞，指「看」(= *look at*)。

6. **B** It is time you <u>began</u> to study.　該是你開始讀書的時候了。

> | *It is time*
It is high time　⎬ + 假設法
It is about time | 【動詞通常用過去式，表示與現在
事實相同，現在極少用 should +
原形，已經不用原形動詞】 |

7. **B** *If I <u>had arrived</u> at the station five minutes earlier*, I could

have caught the train.

如果我早五分鐘到車站，我就可以趕上火車了。

這是典型的「假設法過去式」，與過去事實相反，If 子句用

「過去完成式」，主要子句用 could/should/would/might +

have + p.p.。

8. **B** *If I had worked harder in my twenties,* I would be *much* richer *now.*

如果我 20 幾歲時更努力工作，我現在就會更有錢了。

If 子句中用過去完成式，表示與過去事實相反，主要子句可依情況用任何時態，在此因爲有 now，可知要用假設法現在式 would be，表與現在事實相反。

9. **B** Married men *sometimes* wish they were single.

已婚的男人有時候希望他們是單身。

wish 後用假設法，假設法現在式應用過去式動詞，be 動詞要用 were。

10. **C** I would have been *completely* in despair *if it hadn't been for the help of my friends.*

主詞補語

如果不是因爲我朋友的幫助，我就會完全絕望了。

假設法過去式，應用「過去完成式」表示，本句前後都是假設法過去式。

11. **B** *Should anything happen,* please let us know *immediately.*
= *If anything should happen, …*

萬一任何事發生，請立刻通知我們。

If 省略時，須把助動詞放在主詞前倒裝。

12. **C**　It is essential ***that you be there today.*** 你今天必須在那裡。

凡是 that 子句中需要作「應該」解時，should 大多省略，
這是假設法的現在和未來式，表示「應該做而未做」。

It is $\left\{\begin{array}{l} \textbf{\textit{essential}}（必要的）\\ \textbf{\textit{necessary}}（必須的）\\ \textbf{\textit{important}}（重要的）\\ \vdots \end{array}\right\}$ that + S + (*should*) + V...

13. **D**　I have a friend ***whose** father runs a very nice restaurant*

in this town.

我有一個朋友，他的爸爸在這個鎮上開了一間很好的餐廳。

所有格關代 whose 引導形容詞子句，修飾 friend，在子句
中，whose father 做 runs 的主詞。

14. **C**　The bed *I slept in last night* wasn't *very* comfortable.
我昨晚睡的床不是很舒服。

B. → The bed *in which I slept*【that 不可做介詞受詞】
= The bed (*which*) I slept in
= The bed (*that*) I slept in

15. **D**　***What you should have done*** is (*to*) call the police.
　　　　　名　詞　子　句
你早就該做的事是打電話報警。

What 引導名詞子句，做 is 的主詞，在子句中，What 做 done 的受詞，is 後的 to 常省略，此句型類似：All you have to do is (to) V … 。

16. **C** Reading is *to the mind* **what** exercise is *to the body*.

閱讀之於心靈猶如運動之於身體。

A：B＝C：D　A 之於 B 猶如 C 之於 D。

= A is to B $\begin{cases} \textit{\textbf{what}} \\ \textit{\textbf{as}} \end{cases}$ C is to D.

17. **C** It was getting dark, ***and*** <u>*what*</u> *was worse*, we couldn't find our hotel. 天色越來越黑了，更糟的是，我們找不到飯店。

what was worse 「更糟的是」是插入語，依句意用過去式，現在式為 what is worse。相反的是 what is better「更好的是」。

18. **C** I met a man **who** | *I thought* | was an actor.

插入語

我遇見一個人，我以為是演員。

主格關代和 be 動詞之間可有插入語，插入語動詞通常表看法，如 think, believe, imagine, guess 等。

19. **D** ***If*** <u>*only*</u> I could speak English *as fluently as you*!

要是我英文可以說得和你一樣流利就好了！

> *If only*　但願；要是…就好了！【後接假設法】
> = *O that*
> = *Would that*
> = *I wish*

20. **B** *Having lost* his money, John was not able to pay for lunch.

= *As he had lost his money*, John …

因為約翰錢掉了，他沒辦法付午餐的錢。

完成式分詞構句，表示比主要動詞早發生。

21. **C** *It being* Sunday, the bank was closed.

= *Because* it was Sunday, the bank was closed.

因為是星期天，銀行關門。

前後主詞不同，改分詞構句時應保留主詞。

22. **A** There are still thirty boys *waiting in the room.*

還有 30 個男孩在房裡等待。

There be + S + 分詞，避免重覆，不用形容詞子句形式。

There are … boys *who are* waiting in the room.〔誤〕

23. **C** She sat surrounded by her children.

她坐在那裡，她的小孩圍著她。

$$\left.\begin{array}{l} \text{sit} \\ \text{lie} \\ \text{stand} \\ \text{be} \end{array}\right\} + 分詞,表「被動」用過去分詞。$$

She was surrounded by her children. 【正】

(她被她的孩子圍繞著。)

24. **D** I didn't buy anything *because I didn't see* <u>what I wanted</u>.

名　詞　子　句

我什麼都沒買,因為沒看到我要的東西。

複合關代 *what* 引導名詞子句,做 see 的受詞,在子句中 what 又做 wanted 的受詞。

25. **C** It doesn't matter <u>***whether***</u> *she admits her guilt or not.*

她承不承認她的罪,都不重要。

whether 引導名詞子句,做真正主詞,matter 指「重要」,是完全不及物動詞。

$$\left\{\begin{array}{l} \textit{\textbf{It doesn't matter.}} \ 不重要;沒關係。 \\ = \textit{\textbf{It makes no difference.}} \\ = \textit{\textbf{It's not important.}} \end{array}\right.$$

　　= ***I don't care.*** 我不在乎。

TEST 4

請依照上下文意，選出一個最正確答案，每題 4 分。

1. I wish we had done _____ we were told.
   A. that　　　　　　B. which
   C. as　　　　　　　D. just　　　　　　【奈良女子大】

2. Digital images can be viewed almost immediately,
   _____ films take much longer to develop.
   A. while　　　　　　B. so
   C. because　　　　　D. then　　　　　【武藏工大】

3. You cannot lose weight _____ you give up eating
   between meals.
   A. as long as　　　　B. by the time
   C. until　　　　　　D. while　　　　　【學習院大】

4. A bad habit, _____ formed, cannot easily be gotten
   rid of.
   A. as　　　　　　　B. in
   C. once　　　　　　D. then　　　　　【青山學院大】

5. It is three years _____ he got a driver's license.
   A. after　　　　　　B. since
   C. before　　　　　D. when　　　　　【東京國際大】

6. I had _____ entered the house when the telephone rang.

    A. evenly   B. severely

    C. hardly   D. rarely   【上智大】

7. _____ you are in Paris, you should do some sightseeing and shopping.

    A. Now then

    B. Now that

    C. For now

    D. By now   【東京國際大】

8. _____ he was, he lived happily with his wife.

    A. Poor as

    B. So poor

    C. With poor

    D. Poor since   【東京國際大】

9. _____ you like it or not, you should be here by eight tomorrow morning.

    A. When   B. Whether

    C. Though   D. Even if   【東北工大】

10. The laundry won't dry quickly _____ it's sunny.

    A. if   B. whether

    C. unless   D. since   【七試】

11. Let's take an express train _____ we can get there
20 minutes earlier.

    A. in order   B. so that

    C. such as   D. while   【七試】

12. I think you had better carry an umbrella _____ it
rains.

    A. so that   B. in order that

    C. in case   D. unless   【東邦大】

13. It was _____ a lovely day that everybody felt like
going for a walk.

    A. so   B. such

    C. very   D. as   【東京經濟大】

14. _____ I live, I will not let you do such a thing.

    A. As far as

    B. As long as

    C. As much as

    D. As soon as   【立命館大】

15. _____ work is concerned, I always try to do my best.

    A. So long as

    B. As much as

    C. As soon as

    D. So far as   【大阪產業大】

16. His mother asked him _____ he had been to the bank.
    A. if   B. what
    C. where   D. which   【拓殖大】

17. _____ you pay in cash or by credit card will make no difference.
    A. Although   B. How
    C. Whether   D. If   【松山大】

18. I'm worried _____ she is happy.
    A. as if
    B. in case
    C. about if
    D. about whether   【立命館大】

19. The house _____ he was looking for was on the main street.
    A. where
    B. what
    C. which
    D. in which   【關西學院大】

20. That is the man _____ did it.
    A. as   B. who
    C. whom   D. whose   【上智大】

21. Please inform us _____ any change of address as soon as possible.

    A. in   B. with

    C. of   D. on   【中央大】

22. I regarded him _____ a friend but he betrayed me.

    A. out   B. of

    C. to   D. as   【駒澤大】

23. The traffic jam prevented us _____ on time.

    A. arriving

    B. for arriving

    C. from arriving

    D. of arriving   【東北學院大】

24. He can't _____ right from wrong yet.

    A. say   B. tell

    C. speak   D. talk   【九州國際大】

25. I don't blame you _____ doing that.

    A. for   B. of

    C. with   D. at   【關西外大】

Test 4 詳解

1. **C** I wish we had done ***as*** *we were told.*

   我希望我們能夠<u>依</u>命令行事。

   as（按照）引導副詞子句，修飾 done。

2. **A** Digital images can be viewed *almost immediately,* ***while***

   films take much longer to develop.

   數位影像幾乎可以立刻被看到，<u>然而</u>底片則需要花較長時間沖洗。

   while = whereas = but on the contrary 相反地；然而

   while 看起來是引導副詞子句，但事實上是用來連接兩個對

   等子句，作「然而」解。【詳見「文法寶典」p.471】

   develop 的主要意思是「發展」，在此作「沖洗（底片）」解。

3. **C** You cannot lose weight ***until*** *you give up eating between*

   meals. <u>直到</u>你放棄吃零食，你才能減肥。

   not…until 直到～才…

4. **C** A bad habit, ***once*** *formed,* cannot easily be gotten rid

   of. 壞習慣<u>一旦</u>形成，就不容易被戒除。

   once（一旦）後面省略 it is。

   get rid of「除去」的被動式是 be gotten rid of。

5. **B** It is three years *__since__ he got a driver's license.*

自從他領到駕照以來，已經三年了。

在這裡，It is = It has been。

6. **C** I had *hardly* entered the house *__when__ the telephone rang.*

我一進房間，電話就響了。

$$
\left.\begin{array}{l} \textbf{\textit{hardly}} \\ \textbf{\textit{scarcely}} \end{array}\right\} \cdots \textbf{\textit{when}} \quad \text{一…就～}
$$

先發生用「過去完成式」，後發生用「過去簡單式」，用 hardly（幾乎不），就把前後時間擺平，因此翻成「一…就～」。

7. **B** *__Now that__ you are in Paris*, you should do some sightseeing and shopping.

既然你在巴黎，你應該去觀光和購物。

Now that（既然）引導副詞子句，表「原因」，that 可省略。

8. **A** *__Poor as__ he was*, he lived *happily with his wife*.

雖然他窮，但他和他的太太過得很愉快。

as 在第二個字作「雖然」解。【詳見「文法寶典」p.529】

9. **B** *Whether you like it or not*, you should be here by eight tomorrow morning.

無論你是否喜歡，你都應該在明天早上八點來這裡。

Whether…or not（無論是否…）引導表「讓步」的副詞子句。

10. **C** The laundry won't dry *quickly* **unless** *it's sunny*.

除非有太陽，否則洗的衣服不會很快就乾。

依句意，選 (C) *unless*「除非」。

laundry *n.* 待洗的衣服；剛洗好的衣服

11. **B** Let's take an express train **so that** *we can get there 20 minutes earlier.*

我們搭快車吧，以便於我們能提早二十分鐘到。

so that = in order that = that 可引導表「目的」的副詞子句，子句中可用 can 或 may。

12. **C** I think you had better carry an umbrella **in case** *it rains*.

我認為你最好帶雨傘，以防下雨。

in case (that) = for fear that = lest「以防；以免；為了不」，是表「否定目的」的連接詞，後面可用 should + 原形 V.，或直說法現在式。【詳見「文法寶典」p.514】

這句話也可說成：I think you had better carry an umbrella in case *it should rain*.

13. **B** It was ___*such*___ a lovely day ___*that* everybody felt like going___

___*for a walk.*___ 天氣眞好，所以每個人都要去散步。

___*such…that*___「如此…以致於」，such 是形容詞，後接名詞。

【詳見「文法寶典」p.517】

14. **B** ___*As long as* I live___, I will not let you do such a thing.

只要我活著，我就不會讓你做這種事。

as long as = so long as「只要」，引導副詞子句，表「條件」。

15. **D** ___*So far as* work is concerned___, I ___*always*___ try to do my best.

就工作而言，我總是盡力而爲。

___*so far as…is concerned*___ 就…而言
= *as far as…is concerned*

16. **A** His mother asked him ___*if he had been to the bank.*___

名　詞　子　句

他的媽媽問他是否去過銀行。

ask 後面的 if 子句是名詞子句，if 等於 whether。

17. **C** ___*Whether* you pay *in cash or by credit card*___ will make no

名　詞　子　句

difference. 你付現或刷卡沒什麼差別。

___*whether…or*___ 可引導名詞子句或副詞子句。

18. **D** I'm worried about ***whether she is happy***.

名 詞 子 句

我擔心她是否快樂。

前有介系詞,只能用 whether 引導名詞子句,不可用 if,
故 (C) 用法不合。【詳見「文法寶典」p.485】

19. **C** The house ***which*** *he was looking for* was on the main
street.

= The house *(**that**)* *he was looking for* was on the main
street.

他在找的房子在大街上。

關係代名詞 which 引導形容詞子句,修飾 house,在子句
中做 for 的受詞,which 可以省略或用 that 代替。而
(A) where 在子句中無代名作用。

20. **B** That is the man ***who*** *did it*. 就是那個人做的。

關係代名詞 who 引導形容詞子句,在子句中做 did 的主詞。

21. **C** Please ***inform*** us ***of*** *any* change *of address* as soon as

間受　　　　　直　受

possible. 地址有任何變動,請儘快通知我們。

在中文思想中,「通知某人某事」的「通知」是授與動詞,應
有兩個受詞,但在英文中,有些授與動詞的間接受詞與直接
受詞之間須加 of:

inform（通知）、notify（通知）、
warn（警告）、persuade（說服）、
remind（提醒）、convince（使相信）、 ｝ ＋人＋of＋事
accuse（控告）、cheat（欺騙）、
cure（治療）

【詳見「文法寶典」p.279】

22. **D** I *regarded* him *as* a friend but he betrayed me.

我認為他是朋友，但他卻背叛我。

$$\begin{cases} regard \text{ A } as \text{ B} \quad 認為 A 是 B \\ = look\ upon \text{ A } as \text{ B} \\ = think\ of \text{ A } as \text{ B} \end{cases}$$
$$\begin{cases} = refer\ to \text{ A } as \text{ B} \\ = consider \text{ A } (to\ be) \text{ B} \end{cases}$$

23. **C** The traffic jam *prevented* us *from* arriving on time.

交通阻塞使我們無法準時到達。

$$\begin{cases} prevent\cdots from \quad 阻止\cdots做\sim；使\cdots無法\sim \\ = stop\cdots from \\ = keep\cdots from \end{cases}$$

24. **B** He can't *tell* right *from* wrong yet. 他還無法分辨是非。

$$\begin{cases} tell \text{ A } from \text{ B} \quad 分辨 A 與 B \\ = know \text{ A } from \text{ B} \\ = distinguish \text{ A } from \text{ B} \\ = distinguish\ between \text{ A } and \text{ B} \end{cases}$$

中文：他無法分辨是非。

英文：He can't **tell** right *from* wrong.

　　 = He doesn't **know** right *from* wrong.〔不可用 *can't*〕

　　 = He can't **distinguish** right *from* wrong.

　　 = He can't **distinguish between** right **and** wrong.

25. **A** I don't **blame** you <u>*for*</u> doing that.

我不責備你做那件事。

有些授與動詞的間接受詞與直接受詞之間須加 for：

blame（責備）、ask（要求）、
excuse（原諒）、take（誤認為）、
remember（記得）、forgive（原諒）、
thank（感謝）、scold（責罵）、
mistake（誤認為）、search（尋找）、
punish（處罰）…

+ 人 + for + 事

【詳見「文法寶典」p.280】

【比較】Don't **ask** me *for* help.【正】

　　　 = *Don't ask my help.*【誤】

　　　 Please **excuse** me *for* being late.【正】

　　　 = *Please excuse my being late.*【誤】

　　　 Thank you *for* your help.【正】

　　　 = *Thank your help.*【誤】

TEST 5

請依照上下文意，選出一個最正確答案，每題 4 分。

1. Little _____ seeing you again here.
   A. dream of did I
   B. did I dream of
   C. I dreamed of
   D. I did dream of 【駒澤大】

2. Not only _____ also sick.
   A. she was tired but she was
   B. she was tired but was she
   C. was she tired but she was
   D. was she tired but was she 【福岡大】

3. We don't want to go there, and _____ they.
   A. either do
   B. so do
   C. neither do
   D. neither don't 【關西學院大】

4. He seldom, _____, goes to the movies.
   A. if any
   B. if ever
   C. if impossible
   D. if not 【京都產業大】

5. Those who hunt pandas in China face the death penalty
   if _____.
   A. being caught
   B. caught
   C. having caught
   D. they caught 【慶大】

6. He is not an American _____ a Canadian.
   A. also
   B. so
   C. but
   D. for 【文教大】

7. Some people are rich, while _____ are not.
   A. others
   B. the other
   C. another
   D. their others 【流通科學大】

8. I have four cards here. One is red and _____ are all
   green.
   A. the other
   B. the ones
   C. others
   D. the others 【成城大】

9. Making promises is one thing, keeping them _____.
   A. another
   B. other
   C. others
   D. the others 【高岡法科大】

10. Though they had a heated debate, I kept _____ during the meeting.

    A. quiet   B. quietly

    C. silently   D. talkative   【同志社大】

11. That dream of yours might _____ true some day.

    A. come   B. put

    C. make   D. get   【駒澤大】

12. I'll get him _____ you as soon as he comes home.

    A. call   B. to call

    C. called   D. to be called   【關西學院大】

13. Shall I have him _____ you back later?

    A. be calling   B. call

    C. calling   D. to call   【立命館大】

14. The classroom was so noisy I didn't hear my name _____.

    A. call   B. calling

    C. called   D. to be called   【同志社大】

15. We're supposed to have our new project _____ by Monday.

    A. been finished   B. finish

    C. finished   D. finishing   【東北學院大】

16. My friend ﹍﹍﹍﹍ me some money, which I paid back later on.
    A. lost   B. borrowed
    C. lent   D. presented   【芝浦工大】

17. Neither Jack nor his brothers ﹍﹍﹍﹍ enough money to pay the rent.
    A. has   B. have
    C. are having   D. doesn't have   【同志社大】

18. The number of students who came up with some answer or other ﹍﹍﹍﹍ small.
    A. was   B. were
    C. have been   D. being   【上智大】

19. Not words but action ﹍﹍﹍﹍ now.
    (A) are needed   (B) is needed
    (C) need   (D) needs   【慶應大】

20. ﹍﹍﹍﹍ pigeons are on the platform.
    A. Many a   B. So much
    C. A number of   D. A few of   【九州共立大】

21. Some voted for it; ﹍﹍﹍﹍ voted against it; the rest didn't vote.
    A. other   B. others
    C. the other   D. the others   【四天王寺大】

22. Only when it started to rain _____ that he had left his raincoat somewhere.

    A. did Max notice

    B. noticed Max

    C. did not notice Max

    D. Max did not notice　　　　　　　　【京都外語大】

23. "Frank drives much too fast.　Someday he'll have a terrible accident." "Oh, _____."

    A. I don't hope so

    B. I hope not

    C. I'm not afraid so

    D. I'm afraid not　　　　　　　　　【センター試験】

24. I enjoyed the book and _____.

    A. my wife so did

    B. did so my wife

    C. so did my wife

    D. did my wife so　　　　　　　　　【慶應大】

25. The school is on this side of the river and the church is on _____.

    A. other

    B. the other

    C. another

    D. the another　　　　　　　　　【九州共立大】

Test 5 詳解

1. **B** *Little* <u>did I dream of</u> seeing you *again here*.

   我從來沒想到在此再見到你。

   > little 用於動詞前，指「一點也不」(= *not at all* = *never*)。

   這句話也可以說成：Never did I dream of seeing you again here.

   dream 的主要意思是「夢；作夢；夢想」，dream of 作「想到；認眞考慮」解，常用於否定句。

2. **C** *Not only* <u>was she tired</u> *but* <u>she was</u> *also* sick.

   她不僅很累，而且生病了

   not only 放在句首，主詞和 be 動詞要倒裝，not only…but also 是對等連接詞，also 是副詞，可省略，也可放在句中或句尾。

3. **C** We don't want to go there, *and* <u>neither do</u> they.

   我們不想去那裡，他們也<u>不想去</u>。

   只有答案 (C) 可以補上前面的話，neither do they (*want to go there*)，neither 在此可用 nor 來代替。

   neither 是否定副詞，要倒裝，either 不倒裝，要寫成：and they don't, either.

4. **B** He *seldom*, *if ever*, goes to the movies.

   他即使有也很少去看電影。

if ever, if possible, if any, if not 等是副詞子句的插入，
只是省略主詞和動詞。【詳見「文法寶典」p.653】
我們可以背 seldom, if ever, （即使有也很少），ever 在此
等於 at any time。

5. **B**　Those *who hunt pandas in China* face the death penalty
if (*they are*) _caught_.
在中國捕獵貓熊的人，如果<u>被抓</u>，會面臨死刑的懲罰。

penalty 的意思是「處罰；刑罰；懲罰」，death penalty 是
「死刑；死刑的懲罰」。

6. **C**　He is not an American *but* a Canadian.
他不是美國人，<u>而是</u>加拿大人。

not A but B　不是 A 而是 B

7. **A**　Some people are rich, *while* <u>others</u> are not.
有些人有錢，而<u>另一些人</u>沒有。

some~others　一些~另一些
some~some　一些~一些　　【不指定】
one~another　一個~另一個

8. **D**　I have four cards here.　One is red *and* <u>the others</u> are
all green.　我這裡有四張卡。一張是紅色，<u>其餘的</u>都是綠色。

one~the other　一個~剩下來的一個
one~the others　一個~其餘的　　【指定】

9. **A** Making promises is one thing, keeping them <u>another</u>.

許下承諾是一回事，遵守諾言是<u>另一回事</u>。

本句原為：Making promises is one thing, $\left\{ \begin{array}{l} and \\ but \end{array} \right\}$

keeping them (is) another. 前後呼應，省略對等連接詞 and
或 but，避免重覆，is 省略。***one～another*** 一個～另一個

10. **A** ***Though** they had a heated debate*, I kept <u>quiet</u> *during the*

meeting. 雖然他們的辯論很激烈，我在會議中保持<u>沈默</u>。

keep 在此相當於 be 動詞，後面應接形容詞作主詞補語。
keep quiet 保持沈默 (= *keep silent*)
答案 (D) talkative 多話的，不合句意。

11. **A** That dream *of yours* might <u>come</u> true *some day*.

你的那個夢想有一天可能會<u>成真</u>。

come true 成真 (= *become true*)
come 作「變成」解，請看下例：
Everything will ***come right*** in the end. (一切困難終會過去。)
My shoelaces have ***come undone***. (我的鞋帶鬆開了。)

12. **B** I'll get him <u>to call</u> you *as soon as* *he comes home.*

他一回家，我就叫他<u>打電話給你</u>。

get sb. to V 叫某人作某事 (= *have sb. V*)
本句中，to call you 是不定詞片語，當受詞補語。

13. **B** Shall I have him *call you back later*?

要不要我叫他待會兒回你電話？

have 是使役動詞，接受詞後，接原形動詞作受詞補語。

14. **C** The classroom was *so* noisy *(that) I didn't hear my*

name called. 教室太吵了，我沒有聽到我的名字被叫到。
　　　　受補

感官動詞 hear 接受詞後，接原形動詞表主動，過去分詞表
被動，作受詞補語。so～that「非常～所以」，so 後的詞語
短，可省略 that，也可用逗點（, ）代替。

15. **C** We're supposed to have our new project <u>finished</u> *by*
　　　　　　　　　　　　　　　　　　　　　　　　受補

Monday. 我們應該使我們的新計劃週一前完成。

have* sth. *done 使某事完成（ = *get* sth. *done*）

16. **C** My friend <u>lent</u> me some money, ***which I paid back later***

on. 我的朋友<u>借</u>我一些錢，我後來還了。

later on 後來（ = *later*）

> lend + 間受 + 直受
> borrow + 受詞

***present* sb. *with* sth.** 贈送某人某物

17. **B** *Neither* Jack *nor* his brothers <u>have</u> enough money *to*

pay the rent. 傑克和他的兄弟都沒有足夠的錢付租金。

> *neither A nor B* 做主詞時，動詞和靠近者一致。類似的有：
> Either～or… 不是～就是…
> Not only～but also… 不只～而且…　重點不明確
> 記憶祕訣：重點不明確時，動詞和靠近的主詞一致。

18. **A** The number *of students **who** came up with some answer*

or other <u>was</u> small. 想出某種答案的學生人數很少。

come up with 意思很多，在這裡指「想出 (= *figure out*)；
提出 (= *submit*)」。這個句子不會文法分析，就不知道答案
了，核心主詞是 number，動詞是 was。
some answer or other 某種答案

19. **B** Not words but action <u>is needed</u> *now*.
現在需要的不是說話而是行動。

Not A but B「不是 A 而是 B」做主詞時，重點明確在 B，
動詞與 B 一致。

20. **C** <u>A number of</u> pigeons are on the platform.
好幾隻鴿子在月台上。

a number of「好幾個」，核心主詞是 pigeons，動詞用
複數。

Many a + 單數名詞 + 單數動詞,雖然意義上是複數,因爲
有 a,要用單數,many a 通常用在書寫英文中,口説英文
較少使用。

Many a man ***was*** killed in the war. (許多人在戰爭中喪生。)
沒有 *a few of* (誤) 的用法,因爲 a few 直接可接複數名詞。

21. **B** Some ***voted for*** it; <u>others</u> ***voted against*** it; the rest didn't
vote. 有些人投票贊成;<u>另一些人</u>投票反對;其餘的都沒有投票。

some～others… 一些～另一些… 【參照第 7、8 題】
vote for 投票贊成　　***vote against*** 投票反對

22. **A** ***Only when*** *it started to rain* <u>did Max notice</u> that he had
left his raincoat somewhere.

唯有當開始下雨的時候,麥克斯才注意到,他把雨衣留在某處了。

Only + 副詞 (子句、片語) +
$\left\{\begin{array}{l}助動詞\\be 動詞\end{array}\right\}$
+ 主詞…

23. **B** "Frank drives *much too fast*. *Someday* he'll have a

terrible accident." "Oh, <u>I hope not</u>."

「法蘭克開車開太快了。他總有一天會出嚴重意外的。」
「噢,<u>希望不會</u>。」

so 和 not 在口語中,代替省略句,so 代替肯定句,not 代
替否定句,在此 ***not*** 代替 *that he will **not** have a terrible
accident*。 【詳見「文法寶典」p.646】

24. **C** I enjoyed the book and <u>so did my wife</u>.

我喜歡這本書，<u>我太太也是</u>。

「*so* + 助動詞 + 主詞」表肯定的「也」，否定要用「neither + 助動詞 + 主詞」。so did my wife 源自 so did my wife (*enjoy the book*)。

> 「so + 代名詞 + 助動詞或 be 動詞」，表贊同，如：
> It is hot today. (今天天氣很熱。)
> *So it is*. (是的，是很熱。) (= *Yes, it is.*)

25. **B** The school is on this side *of the river **and*** the church is on <u>the other</u>. 學校在河的這一邊，教堂在<u>另一邊</u>。

表示「一個～另一個…」，本來是 *one～the other*…，這條題目用 this 代替 one，這個句子可改成：…is on *one* side… and…*the other*，爲避免重覆，the other 後省略 side。

【劉毅老師的話】

　　不論你做多少文法題目，不小心總會有錯，我們新發明的「一口氣考試英語」，將試題編成會話，同學背了，做起題目來更快，甚至不用思考，就可答題。

TEST 6

請依照上下文意，選出一個最正確答案，每題 4 分。

1. I have _____ for you.

   A. an information interested

   B. an interesting piece of information

   C. informations interesting

   D. interesting informations 【七試】

2. You won't find _____ news in today's paper.

   A. some　　　　　B. a

   C. much　　　　　D. many 【玉川大】

3. A policeman caught me _____ arm.

   A. with my

   B. by the

   C. by any

   D. with the 【流通經濟大】

4. I never heard _____ story.

   A. such a strange

   B. so strange an

   C. a so strange

   D. so a strange 【大阪產業大】

5. You can rent a bicycle _____ the hour at this shop.

    A. at   B. by

    C. in   D. to   【姬路獨協大】

6. Our task is to finish the work within a couple of hours, _____?

    A. aren't we   B. doesn't it

    C. don't we   D. isn't it   【上智大】

7. Bill _____ ever played the drums, has he?

    A. can't have

    B. won't have

    C. hasn't

    D. hadn't   【聖心女子大】

8. Come and stay with us for the weekend, _____?

    A. do you

    B. won't you

    C. aren't you

    D. don't you   【東海大】

9. Let's go fishing at the lake tomorrow, _____?

    A. will we   B. shall we

    C. don't you   D. let we   【東洋大】

10. What are you going to do _____ Saturday evening?
      A. at   B. into
      C. on   D. to   【帝塚山學院大】

11. The deadline is 6 p.m. I must finish this work _____
      that time.
      A. till   B. by
      C. to   D. in   【青山學院大】

12. I have been living in Canada _____ almost five
      years.
      A. since   B. while
      C. during   D. for   【拓殖大】

13. I'll be back _____ ten minutes.
      A. at   B. in
      C. after   D. before   【愛知工大】

14. She was so tired that she fell asleep with her socks
      _____.
      A. at   B. by
      C. in   D. on   【九州產業大】

15. _____ her great surprise, her uncle failed in his
      business.
      A. At   B. To
      C. For   D. From   【佛教大】

16. The task is _____ much importance to them.

    A. with   B. at

    C. in   D. of   【近畿大】

17. Jane is younger than him _____ five years.

    A. at   B. by

    C. for   D. with   【實踐女子大】

18. He came to the party _____ his illness.

    A. though

    B. although

    C. in spite

    D. despite   【和光大】

19. The man _____ the blue suit is Mr. Brown.

    A. on   B. to wearing

    C. putting   D. in   【聖學院大】

20. This sweater is better, but it costs _____ the other

    one.

    A. as much twice as

    B. twice as much as

    C. as twice much as

    D. twice more than   【關東學院大】

21. She is not _____ an actress as a singer.
    A. as beautiful B. so beautiful
    C. as such D. so much 【早大】

22. The Amazon is _____ than the Mississippi.
    A. the longest
    B. as long
    C. more longer
    D. much longer 【拓殖大】

23. His paper is superior _____.
    A. than mine B. to mine
    C. than me D. to me 【東海大】

24. "I have at most 100 dollars." means "I have _____ 100 dollars."
    A. more than
    B. less than
    C. not more than
    D. not less than 【大谷女子大】

25. Tom is taller than _____ in his class.
    A. every boy else
    B. all the other boy
    C. any other boys
    D. any other boy 【獨協醫大】

Test 6 詳解

1. **B** I have <u>an interesting piece of information</u> for you.
我有一個有趣的消息要告訴你。

information「資訊；消息」是抽象名詞，不可數，只能用
單位名詞 a piece of 表「數」的觀念，形容詞應加在單位
名詞前。

I have information for you.（我有消息要告訴你。）
I have a piece of interesting information for you.【誤】

2. **C** You won't find <u>much</u> news *in today's paper.*
今天的報紙裡沒什麼新聞。

news「新聞；消息」是不可數名詞，常考的還有：
knowledge（知識）、homework（家庭作業）、money
（錢）、advice（忠告）、furniture（家具）等。

3. **B** A policeman caught me <u>by the</u> arm. 警察抓住我的手臂。

> *catch sb. by the arm* 抓住某人的手臂
> = take *sb.* by *the* arm
> = hold *sb.* by *the* arm
> = grasp *sb.* by *the* arm

pat *sb.* on *the* shoulder 拍某人的肩膀
strike *sb.* on *the* head 打某人的頭
= hit *sb.* on *the* head

「動詞＋某人＋介詞＋*the*＋某人身體一部分」，the 不可
改成所有格。【詳見「文法寶典」p.277】

4. **A** I never heard <u>such a strange</u> story.

我從來沒聽過這麼奇怪的故事。

(B) 應改成 so strange a，即使如此，現在美國人極少用。

5. **B** You can rent a bicycle ***by the hour*** *at this shop.*

在這家店裡，你可以按小時租腳踏車。

> *by* + *the* + 單位名詞
> ⎧ ***by the day*** 按日
> ⎨ ***by the week*** 按週
> ⎩ ***by the month*** 按月

6. **D** Our task is to finish the work *within a couple of hours,*
isn't it?

我們的任務，是在幾小時之內完成這項工作，<u>不是嗎</u>？

「句尾附加句」的秘訣在於，它是一個簡單形式的省略疑問句，這裡的 isn't it 是 isn't it (*to finish…*)。

a couple of 很多人搞不清楚到底是幾個，根據 Macmillan English Dictionary，在英國，a couple of 幾乎總是指「兩個」，在美國，可以指「兩個」，也常指「不定的幾個」（= *a few*）。

7. **C** Bill <u>hasn't</u> ever played the drums, ***has he***?

比爾從來沒有打過鼓，有嗎？

句尾附加句肯定，主要子句要用否定，has he 是 has he ever played… 的省略。ever「曾經」用於否定和疑問句中，相當於 at any time。

8. **B**　Come ***and*** stay with us *for the weekend, **won't you**?*

來和我們一起過週末，好不好啊？

肯定命令句後的句尾附加句，表「請求」用 ***will you***?，表「邀請」用 ***won't you***?【詳見「文法寶典」p.6】

9. **B**　Let's go fishing *at the lake tomorrow, **shall we**?*

我們明天到湖邊釣魚，好不好啊？

Let's 引導的命令句，肯定用 ***shall we***?，否定用 ***all right***? 或 ***OK***?【詳見「文法寶典」p.6】

10. **C**　What are you going to do *on Saturday evening*?

你星期六晚上打算做什麼？

特定日期的早、午、晚，介系詞用 on。

【比較】　in the evening　在晚上
　　　　　on Saturday evening　在星期六晚上【特定】

　　　　　in the morning　在早上
　　　　　on the morning of April 15
　　　　　在 4 月 15 日早上【特定】

　　　　　at night　在晚上
　　　　　on a dark night　在一個漆黑的晚上【特定】

11. **B** The deadline is 6 p.m. I must finish this work *by that*

time.

最後期限是下午六點鐘。我必須在那之前完成這個工作。

by 表「最遲在…之前」，*till* 表「直到」，意思不同。

【比較】 ⎰ I'll be here *by* 6 o'clock. (我最遲六點鐘到。)
⎱ = I'll arrive before 6 o'clock.

I'll be here *till* 6 o'clock.
(我會在這待到六點鐘。)
= I'll leave at 6 o'clock.

12. **D** I have been living in Canada *for almost five years*.

我在加拿大住了將近五年了。

for 表「持續一段時間」，通常和「完成式」或「完成進行式」連用，during 指「在～期間」。

13. **B** I'll be back *in ten minutes*. 我再過十分鐘就回來了。

in 表「再過～」，after 表「經過～之後」。

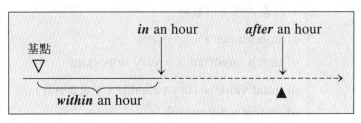

14. **D** She was *so* tired ***that*** *she fell asleep with her socks <u>on</u>*.

她太累了，所以穿著襪子就睡著了。

「with + 受詞 + 受詞補語」表伴隨主要動詞的情況，這裡的 on 源自 put on（穿上），如：She put on her socks.（她穿上襪子。）

15. **B** <u>*To her great surprise*</u>, her uncle failed in his business.

想不到，他的叔叔做生意失敗了。

to her surprise 字面的意思是「令她驚訝的是」，在這裡作「想不到」解。to 常與情感名詞連用，如：to *one's* disappointment（令某人失望的是），to *one's* shame（令某人丟臉的是），to *one's* joy（令某人高興的是），to *one's* relief（令某人放心的是），to *one's* sorrow（令某人悲傷的是），to *one's* dismay（令某人驚慌的是）。【詳見「文法寶典」p.601】

16. **D** The task is <u>of</u> much importance to them.

那個任務對他們很重要。

of + 抽象名詞 = 形容詞

$$\begin{cases} \text{of importance} = \text{important} \\ \text{of much importance} = \text{very important} \end{cases}$$

$$\begin{cases} \text{of great value} = \text{very valuable}（很有價值的） \\ \text{of no use} = \text{not useful} \end{cases}$$

【詳見「文法寶典」p.69】

17. **B** Jane is younger *than him <u>by</u> five years*.

珍比他年輕五歲。

by 表「差距」。【詳見「文法寶典」p.566】

這句話也可説成：Jane is five years younger than him.
現代英語中，已經將 than 後的主格 he 改成 him，除非後
面是完整的句子，像：Jane is five years younger than
he is.

18. **D** He came to the party <u>despite</u> his illness.

<u>儘管</u>他生病，他還是來參加宴會。

despite *prep.* 儘管（= *in spite of*）

19. **D** The man <u>*in*</u> *the blue suit* is Mr. Brown.

<u>穿著藍色西裝</u>的那個男人是布朗先生。

in 表「穿著」（= *wearing* = *dressed in*）。

這句話也可説成：The man ***wearing*** the blue suit is Mr.
Brown. 或 The man ***dressed in*** the blue suit is Mr.
Brown.

put on 雖然作「穿上」解，但表「動作」，如：He put
on a sweater because it was getting cold.（因爲天氣變
冷，所以他穿上毛衣。）

20. **B** …, but it costs *<u>twice as much as</u> the other one*.

這件毛衣比較好，但是它的價格<u>是</u>另一件的<u>兩倍</u>。

　　倍數副詞的表達法：表示「什麼是什麼的幾倍」。

$\left\{\begin{array}{l}倍數＋as＋形容詞或副詞＋as…\\倍數＋the＋名詞＋of＋…\end{array}\right.$

【詳見「文法寶典」p.182】

21. **D** She is *not so much* an actress *as* a singer.

與其說她是女演員，不如說她是歌手。

$\left\{\begin{array}{l}\textbf{\textit{not so much}} \text{ A } \textbf{\textit{as}} \text{ B }\quad 與其說是 A，不如說是 B\\=\textbf{\textit{not}}\text{ A }\textbf{\textit{but}}\text{ B}\\=\text{B }\textbf{\textit{rather than}}\text{ A}\end{array}\right.$

這句話也可說成：She is a singer *rather than* an actress.
（她是一個歌手，而不是女演員。）或 She is *not* an actress
but a singer.（她不是女演員，而是歌手。）

22. **D** The Amazon is *much* longer *than the Mississippi.*

亞馬遜河比密西西比河長多了。

much 修飾比較級，very 修飾原級。

23. **B** His paper is superior to mine.

他的報告比我的報告好。

paper 在此可作「紙」或「報告」解。

$\left\{\begin{array}{l}\text{be superior to }\ 優於\\\text{be inferior to }\ 劣於\end{array}\right.$

$\left\{\begin{array}{l}\text{be senior to }\ 比～年長\\\text{be junior to }\ 比～年輕\end{array}\right.$

字尾是 ior，比較級不用 than，而用 to。

依句意，mine = my paper，不可用 to me，因爲「同類才能相比」。

24. **C** "I have *at most* 100 dollars." means "I have <u>not more than</u> 100 dollars."

「我最多有 100 元。」意思是「我的錢<u>不超過</u> 100 元。」

> *not more than* 不超過；最多 (= *at most*)
> *not less than* 不少於；至少 (= *at least*)
>
> 　　【詳見「文法寶典」p.202】

25. **D** Tom is taller *than <u>any other boy</u> in his class.*

湯姆比班<u>上任何一個其他的</u>男孩都高。

比較須將自己除外，「任何其他的」是 any other，後可接單數或複數名詞，因爲主詞 Tom 是單數，所以用單數的 boy，選 (D)。

> 【比較】Tom is taller than *any* boy in the neighboring class.
>
> 　　湯姆比隔壁班任何男孩都高。
>
> 　　【正，自身已除外，不必再加 other】
>
> 　　【詳見「文法寶典」p.208】

TEST 7

1. The reports went missing in 2012 and nobody _____ them since.
   A. sees　　　　　　　B. saw
   C. has seen　　　　　D. was seen 　　　　【2014年全國大綱】

2. _____ me tomorrow and I'll let you know the lab result.
   A. Calling　　　　　B. Call
   C. To call　　　　　D. Having called 　　【2014年全國大綱】

3. Henry was away from home for quite a bit and _____ saw his family.
   A. frequently　　　　B. seldom
   C. always　　　　　　D. usually 　　　　【2014年全國大綱】

4. — What did you do last weekend?
   — Oh, nothing _____.
   A. much　　　　　　B. else
   C. ever　　　　　　　D. yet 　　　　　　【2014年全國大綱】

5. There are still many problems _____ before we are ready for a long stay on the moon.
   A. solving　　　　　B. solved
   C. being solved　　　D. to be solved 　　　【2014年北京】

6. _____ the forest park is far away, a lot of tourists visit it every year.
   A. As   B. When
   C. Even though   D. In case   【2014年北京】

7. The best moment for the football star was _____ he scored the winning goal.
   A. where   B. when
   C. how   D. why   【2014年北京】

8. The book has helped me greatly in my daily communication, especially at work, _____ a good impression is a must.
   A. which   B. when
   C. as   D. where   【2014年江蘇】

9. Tom always goes jogging in the morning, and he usually does push-ups to stay _____.
   A. in place   B. in order
   C. in shape   D. in fashion   【2014年江蘇】

10. I can't meet you on Sunday. I'll be _____ occupied.
    A. also   B. just
    C. nevertheless   D. otherwise   【2014年江蘇】

11. The lecture _____, a lively question-and-answer session followed.
    A. was given　　　　　B. having given
    C. to be given
    D. having been given　　　　　【2014 年江蘇】

12. — _____! Somebody has left the lab door open.
    — Don't look at me.
    A. Dear me　　　　　B. Hi, there
    C. Thank goodness　　D. Come on　　【2014 年江蘇】

13. The exact year _____ Angela and her family spent together in China was 2008.
    A. when　　　　　B. where
    C. why　　　　　D. which　　【2014 年安徽】

14. The twins, who _____ their homework, were allowed to play badminton on the playground.
    A. will finish　　　B. finish
    C. have finished　　D. had finished　【2014 年安徽】

15. You can ask anyone for help. _____ here is willing to lend you a hand.
    A. One　　　　　B. No one
    C. Everyone　　　D. Someone　　【2014 年安徽】

16. The meaning of the word "nice" changed a few times _____ it finally came to include the sense "pleasant".

    A. before   B. after

    C. since   D. while   【2014 年安徽】

17. Terry, please _____ your cell phone when Grandma is talking to you.

    A. look up from   B. look into

    C. look back on   D. look through   【2014 年安徽】

18. When the sports hero _____ at our party, he was welcomed with open arms.

    A. turned up   B. left off

    C. moved on   D. got away   【2014 年安徽】

19. While waiting for the opportunity to get _____, Henry did his best to peform his duty.

    A. promote   B. promoted

    C. promoting   D. to promote   【2014 年安徽】

20. It's our hope that we will play a greater role in the marketplace and, _____, supply more jobs.

    A. however   B. anywhere

    C. therefore   D. otherwise   【2014 年安徽】

21. Shakespeare's writing is still popular today. It has really _____ the test of time.
    A. failed   B. stood
    C. taken   D. conducted   【2014年安徽】

22. They chose Tom to be _____ captain of the team because they knew he was _____ smart leader.
    A. a ; the   B. the ; the
    C. the ; a   D. a ; a   【2014年江西】

23. Thanks for your directions to the house; we wouldn't have found it _____.
    A. nowhere   B. however
    C. otherwise   D. instead   【2014年江西】

24. Starting your own business could be a way to achieve financial independence. _____, it could just put you in debt.
    A. In other words   B. All in all
    C. As a result
    D. On the other hand   【2014年江西】

25. _____ nearly all our money, we couldn't afford to stay at a hotel.
    A. Having spent   B. To spend
    C. Spent   D. To have spent   【2014年江西】

26. — When shall I call, in the morning or afternoon?

    — _____. I'll be in all day.

    A. Any   B. None

    C. Neither   D. Either   【2014 年江西】

27. He is thought _____ foolishly. Now he has no one but himself to blame for losing the job.

    A. to act   B. to have acted

    C. acting   D. having acted   【2014 年江西】

28. It was the middle of the night _____ my father woke me up and told me to watch the football game.

    A. that   B. as

    C. which   D. when   【2014 年江西】

29. Children, when _____ by their parents, are allowed to enter the stadium.

    A. to be accompanied

    B. to accompany   C. accompanying

    D. accompanied   【2014 年湖南】

30. If Mr. Dewey _____ present, he would have offered any possible assistance to the people there.

    A. were   B. had been

    C. should be   D. was   【2014 年湖南】

31. — I've prepared all kinds of food for the picnic.

 — Do you mean we _____ bring anything with us?

 A. can't　　　　　　　B. mustn't

 C. hasn't　　　　　　　D. needn't　　　　【2014年湖南】

32. You will never gain successs _____ you are fully devoted to your work.

 A. when　　　　　　　B. because

 C. after　　　　　　　D. unless　　　　【2014年湖南】

33. There is no greater pleasure than lying on my back in the middle of the grassland, _____ at the night sky.

 A. to stare　　　　　　B. staring

 C. stared　　　　　　　D. having stared　　【2014年湖南】

34. Since the time humankind started gardening, we _____ to make our environment more beautiful.

 A. try　　　　　　　　B. have been trying

 C. are trying　　　　　　D. will try　　　【2014年湖南】

35. _____ what you're doing today important, because you're trading a day of your life for it.

 A. Make　　　　　　　B. To make

 C. Making　　　　　　　D. Made　　　　【2014年湖南】

36. It's not doing the things we like, but liking the things
   we have to do _____ makes life happy.
   A. that   B. how
   C. what   D. who   【2014 年湖南】

37. _____ ourselves from physical and mental tensions,
   we each need deep thought and inner peace.
   A. Having freed   B. Freed
   C. To free   D. Freeing   【2014 年湖南】

38. I've been trying to phone Charles all evening, but there
   must be something wrong with the network; I can't seem
   to _____.
   A. get through   B. get off
   C. get in   D. get along   【2014 年湖北】

39. Is this your necklace, Mary? I _____ it when I was
   cleaning the bathroom this morning.
   A. came across   B. dealt with
   C. looked after   D. went for   【2014 年湖北】

40. Check carrots, potatoes, onions and any other vegetables
   _____, and immediately use or throw away any
   which show signs of rotting.
   A. in demand   B. in storage
   C. on loan   D. on sale   【2014 年湖北】

41. _____ you start eating in a healthier way, weight control will become much easier.
    A. Unless　　　　　 B. Although
    C. Before　　　　　 D. Once　　　　　【2014 年天津】

42. _____ the school, the village has a clinic, which was also built with government support.
    A. In reply to
    B. In addition to
    C. In charge of
    D. In place of　　　　　【2014 年天津】

43. Clearly and thoughtfully _____, the book inspires confidence in students who wish to seek their own answers.
    A. writing　　　　　 B. to write
    C. written　　　　　 D. being written　　　　　【2014 年天津】

44. English is a language shared by several diverse cultures, _____ uses it differently.
    A. all of which　　　　　 B. each of which
    C. all of them　　　　　 D. each of them　　　　　【2014 年天津】

45. The two countries will meet to _____ trade barriers.
    A. make up　　　　　 B. use up
    C. turn down　　　　　 D. break down　　　　　【2014 年天津】

46. I think _____ impresses me about his painting is the colors he uses.

    A. what   B. that

    C. which   D. who   【2014 年天津】

47. It's quite hot today. Do you feel like _____ for a swim?

    A. to go   B. going

    C. go   D. having gone   【2014 年陝西】

48. The Scottish girl _____ blue eyes won the first prize in the Fifth Chinese Speech Contest.

    A. by   B. of

    C. in   D. with   【2014 年陝西】

49. Unless some extra money _____, the theater will close.

    A. was found   B. finds

    C. is found   D. found   【2014 年全國大綱】

50. _____ village where I was born has grown into _____ town.

    A. The ; a   B. A ; the

    C. The ; the   D. A ; a   【2014 年陝西】

Test 7 詳解

1. **C** 報告書在 2012 年遺失了，從那以後，就沒有人再<u>看到</u>。

    since 在此是副詞，作「從那以後；此後；後來」解時，和「現在完成式」連用。

    但 ***since*** 作「之前；以前」解時，則和「過去式」連用，如：He disappeared many years ***since***.

    （他許多年前就不知去向。）

2. **B** <u>如果你明天打電話給我</u>，我就會告訴你實驗室的結果。

    命令句也可表「條件」，and 表「肯定」，or 表「否定」。

    全句等於：If you call me tomorrow, I'll let you know the lab result.

    lab *n.* 實驗室（ = *laboratory*） *adj.* 實驗室的

3. **B** 亨利很多時間都不在家，<u>很少</u>見到家人。

    依句意，選 (B) *seldom*「很少」。

    quite a bit, ***quite a lot***, ***quite a few*** 都作「很多；大量」解，在這裡 quite a bit 是指 quite a bit of time（很多時間）。

4. **A** —— 你上週末做了什麼？

    —— 喔，<u>沒做什麼事</u>。

    nothing much 沒什麼

    $\begin{cases} = \text{nothing important} \quad 沒什麼重要的 \\ = \text{nothing special} \quad 沒什麼特別的 \\ = \text{nothing worth mentioning} \quad 沒什麼值得提的 \end{cases}$

5. **D** 在我們做好準備，去月球上長期停留之前，仍然有許多問題<u>要</u>
<u>解決</u>。

… many problems *to be solved* ….

不定詞片語當形容詞用，修飾 problems。

不定詞表「未來」，分詞暗示「已有的經驗」。

6. **C** <u>即使</u>森林公園很遠，每年仍然有很多觀光客去遊覽。

依句意，選 (C) *Even though*「即使」。

7. **B** The best moment *for the football star* was ***when*** he
scored the winning goal. 對那位足球明星而言，最輝煌
的時刻，就是<u>當</u>他踢進致勝的一球時。

when 引導名詞子句做補語。　　goal *n.* 得分進球；目標

8. **D** 這本書對於我日常的溝通大有幫助，尤其是在辦公室，必須給
人留下好的印象。

…, especially at work ***where*** *a good impression is a must.*

at work ①在工作地點（ = *at the place where you work* ）

②在工作時（ = *in the process of doing or making*
something ）

at work 在此是指「在工作地點；在辦公室」，故用 where
引導形容詞子句。

must *n.* 絕對需要之物；必備之物

9. **C** 湯姆早上一定會去慢跑，而且通常會做伏地挺身保持<u>健康</u>。

stay in shape 保持健康　　push-up *n.* 伏地挺身

原題是… does push-ups too to stay…，too 去掉較佳，
避免和同音的 to 在一起。

10. **D** 禮拜天我沒辦法見你。我有<u>別的事</u>要忙。

otherwise *adv.* ①否則 ②別種方式 ③在其他方面

occupy *v.* 佔據；使忙碌

I'll be otherwise occupied. 我有別的事要忙。

= I'll be occupied elsewhere.

= I'll be busy in other respects.

= I'll be doing something different.

用 *otherwise* 是一種比較有禮貌的說法，單獨只說 *I'll be occupied.*（我會很忙。）較不禮貌。

11. **D** 演講結束後，接著是熱烈的問答時間。

After the lecture had been given, a ⋯

= The lecture *having been given*, a ⋯

副詞子句→分詞構句：

①去連接詞。②主詞不相同，保留。③ V → V-ing。

lively *adj.* 活潑的；（討論）熱烈的

question-and-answer session 問答時間

12. **A** ─ <u>哎呀</u>！有人沒關實驗室的門。

─ 不要看我。

> A. *Dear me!* 哎呀！；天啊！
> - = My God!.
> - = My goodness!
> - = Oh, my goodness!
> - = Goodness!
> - = Heavens!
> - = Goodness gracious!
>
> 【按照使用頻率排列】

B. Hi, there! 嗨！(= *Hi!* = *Hello!*)

C. Thank goodness! 感謝上帝！
(= *Thank God!* = *That's good!*)

D. Come on! 快點！；振作起來！；得了吧！；來呀！；
動手呀！

13. **D** 安琪拉和她家人在中國一起度過的那一年，正是 2008 年。

The exact year ***which*** *Angela and her family spent*
                                                 vt.

together in China was 2008.

乍看之下，答案好像是 when，但其實要用 which，因為
which 代替 the exact year，做 spent 的受詞。

spent 是及物動詞，應有受詞，例如：They spent a whole
year together in China. (他們在中國度過了一整年。)

14. **D** 這對雙胞胎做完了功課，可以去操場打羽毛球。

過去的過去，用「過去完成式」。

15. **C** 你可以要求任何人協助。這裡的每個人都願意幫助你。

依句意，選 (C) *Everyone*。

lend *sb.* ***a hand*** 幫助某人 (= *help sb.*)

16. **A** nice 這個字的意思改變了很多次，最後才包括「令人愉快的」
意思。

依句意，選 (A) *before*。

sense *n.* 意義

17. **A** 泰瑞，當祖母和你說話時，請<u>抬頭不要看</u>手機。

look up 往上看

Terry, please look up *from your cell phone….*

(B) look into「調查」，(C) look back on「回顧」，

(D) look through「透過⋯看」，則不合句意。

18. **A** 當那位運動明星<u>出現</u>在我們的宴會時，受到熱烈的歡迎。

依句意，選 (A) ***turn up***「出現」(= *appear*)。而

(B) leave off「停止 (做某事)」，(C) move on「繼續前

進」，(D) get away「離開」，則不合句意。

with open arms 熱烈地 (歡迎等)

19. **B** 亨利在等待<u>升遷</u>機會的期間，盡力做好他的職責。

… opportunity *to get <u>promoted</u>, ….*

promote *v.* 升職　　***get promoted*** 得到晉升

perform *one's* ***duty*** 盡職 (= *do one's duty*)

20. **C** 我們希望能在市場上扮演更重要的角色，<u>因此</u>就能提供更多的
工作機會。

marketplace *n.* 市場 (= *market*)

依句意，選 (C) ***therefore***「因此」。

21. **B** 莎士比亞的作品現在仍然受人歡迎。它<u>經得起時間的考驗</u>。

stand the test of time 經得起時間的考驗

一般情況下，stand 作「站」解，在此作「經得起」解。

writing *n.* 著作

22. **C** 他們選湯姆為隊長，因為他們知道他是個聰明的領導者。

the captain *of the team*「隊長」，「特定」要用 *the*。
a smart leader「一個聰明的領導者」，不指定，用 a。

23. **C** 謝謝你告訴我們那間房子的方向；<u>否則</u>我們會找不到。
依句意，選 (C) *otherwise*「否則」。【詳見「文法寶典」
p.367 , p.474】

24. **D** 開始做自己的事業，可能是獲得財務獨立的方法。<u>另一方面</u>，
這樣也可能使你負債。
依句意，選 (D) *On the other hand*「另一方面；然而」
(= *However* = *Nevertheless* = *Nonetheless* = *Yet*)。
而 (A) in other words「換句話說」，(B) all in all「總
之」，(C) as a result「因此」，皆不合句意。

25. **A** 因為我們<u>已經</u>幾乎花光所有的錢，所以我們住不起飯店。
Having spent nearly all our money, we....
= *As we had spent* nearly all our money, we....
完成式的分詞，表示比主要動詞早發生。

26. **D** ── 我該什麼時候打電話，早上還是下午？
── <u>都可以</u>。我整天都在家。
依句意，選 (D) *Either*「兩者中任一」。而 (A) any「三者
以上任一」，(B) none「三者以上無一」，(C) neither「兩
者中沒有一個」，則不合句意。　　*be in* 在家

27. **B** 他被認為行為愚蠢。現在他失去工作，不能怪別人，只能怪他自己。

He is thought <u>to have acted foolishly</u>.
　　　　　　　　不定詞片語當主詞補語

「完成式不定詞」表比主要動作先發生。【詳見「文法寶典」p.423】

28. **D** 半夜的時候，我的父親把我叫醒，叫我去看足球賽。

It was the middle of the night ***when*** *my father woke*
me up ....

when 引導形容詞子句，修飾 the middle of the night「半夜」。

如果是 It is ... that 的強調句型，則須加 in，寫成：
It was in the middle of the night ***that*** ....

29. **D** 有父母親陪伴時，孩子才被允許進入體育館。

when accompanied 源自 when *they are* accompanied。
從屬連接詞 when, if, while, as 等引導的副詞子句，句意明確時，可省略主詞和 be 動詞。【詳見「文法寶典」p.645】

30. **B** 如果杜威先生在場，他就會提供在那裡的人，任何可能的協助。
假設法的過去式，與過去事實相反，if 子句應該用「過去完成式」的形式，故選 (B) ***had been***。

31. **D** ── 我已經準備好野餐的各種食物。
　　── 你的意思是說，我們<u>不需要</u>帶任何東西嗎？
依句意，選 (D) ***needn't***「不需要」。

32. **D** 除非你全心投入工作，否則你永遠不會成功。

依句意，選 (D) *unless*「除非」。

be devoted to 專心於；致力於

33. **B** 沒有什麼比平躺在草地中間凝視著夜空，還要來得快樂。

一句話講完之後，接著分詞構句，表示對前面所說的話
加以補充，也表示和主要意義的動詞同時的動作。

lie on one's *back* 平躺　　*lie on* one's *side* 側躺

lie on one's *stomach* 趴著；俯臥

34. **B** 自從人類開始栽培花木以來，就一直努力想讓環境變得更漂亮。

since 子句用過去式，主要子句用「現在完成式」或「現
在完成進行式」，故選 (B) *have been trying*。

garden〔ˋgɑrdn〕*v.* 造園；栽培花木；從事園藝

35. **A** 要重視你今天所做的事情，因為這是你用生命中的一天時間換
來的。

Make	what you're doing today	important
	受　　詞	受詞補語

字面的意思是「把你今天所做的事情變得重要」，引申為「要
重視你今天所做的事情」。

命令句應用原形動詞 Make。　　*trade…for*~　以…交換~

36. **A** 要使人生快樂的方法，不是做自己喜歡做的事，而是喜歡自己必
須做的事。

這句話如果把 It's 和 that 去掉，還是完整句，此時就知道，
這句話是「強調句型」，故選 (A) *that*。

Not doing the things *we like but* liking the

things *we have to do* makes life happy.

Not A but B「不是 A 而是 B」，動詞和 B 一致。

這句話也可寫成：

We can make life happy *not by* doing the things we like *but by* liking the things we have to do.

37. **C** 為了使我們自己免除身體和心理的緊張，我們每個人都需要深思和內心的平靜。

不定詞片語修飾 need，表「目的」。

free A *from* B 使 A 免於 B

38. **A** 我整個晚上一直想打電話給查爾斯，但電話網路一定有問題；我似乎無法接通。

A. *get through* 接通（電話）（= *reach*）
B. get off 下（車）
C. get in 上（車） D. get along 進展

39. **A** 這是你的項鍊嗎，瑪麗？我今天早上打掃浴室時，偶然發現它。

A. *come across* 偶然發現（= *find…by chance*）；偶然遇見
B. deal with 應付；處理
C. look after 照顧 D. go for 競爭；追求

40. **B** 檢查庫存的胡蘿蔔、馬鈴薯、洋蔥，和任何其他的蔬菜，凡是有腐爛跡象的，就要立刻使用或丟棄。

依句意，選 (B) *in storage*「儲存的」。原題的 (B) 是 in
store，不常用，因為容易和 in the store 搞混，故改成
in storage，也可改成 you have stored。

而 (A) in demand「需求量大」，(C) on loan「暫借的」，
(D) on sale「廉價出售」，則不合句意。

…any ***which*** *show signs of rotting.*

41. D ***Once*** *you start eating in a healthier way,* weight

control will become *much* easier.

一旦你開始吃得比較健康，體重控制就變得容易多了。

依句意，選 (D) ***Once***「一旦」，表條件。

42. B *In addition to the school,* the village has a clinic,

which *was also built with government support.*

除了學校以外，村裡還有一家診所，也是由政府贊助興建的。

in addition to 除了～以外（還有）(= *besides*)

with government support 意思是 with money *given by*

the government（用政府給的錢）。

43. C 因為這本書寫得很清楚、考慮周到，它激發了學生的信心，想
要自己尋找答案。

As it is clearly and thoughtfully written, the book....

= Clearly and thoughtfully <u>written</u>, the book....

副詞子句改成分詞構句：去連接詞，去相同主詞，碰到 being 或 having been 要省略，故選 (C) *written*。

44. **B** English is the language *shared by several diverse*

*cultures, <u>each of **which**</u> uses it differently.*

英文這種語言，由數個不同的文化群體共同使用，<u>每一個群體</u>使用的方式都不同。

這句話意思是：英語在許多不同的地方被使用，各地的人們都有他們特有的不同口音和字彙。

English is spoken in many different places by people who have different accents and vocabulary specific to their societies.

each of which 引導形容詞子句，修飾 cultures，在子句中做 uses 的主詞，因為是單數動詞，不能用 (A) all of which。each of which 的用法，詳見「文法寶典」p.154，關係代名詞與介詞。

45. **D** 這兩個國家將會會面，以<u>消除</u>貿易的障礙。

依句意，選 (D) *break down*「拆除；打破；消除」。而 (A) make up「組成」，(B) use up「用完」，(C) turn down「拒絕」，則不合句意。

原題是：The *two* countries are going *to* meet *to* break down some barriers *to* trade between them.

這個句子有四個字的音相同，包含一個 two 和三個 to，
不符合美國人的造句習慣。

46. **A**　I think ***what*** *impresses me about his painting* is the

colors *he uses.*　我認為他的畫讓我印象深刻的是他用的顏色。
what 引導名詞子句，做 think 的受詞，在子句中，又做
impresses 的主詞。複合關代 what = the thing that。

47. **B**　今天很熱。你想不想去游泳？
feel like + V-ing　想要
go for a swim　去游泳（= *go swimming*）

48. **D**　有藍色眼睛的蘇格蘭女孩，在第五屆中文演講比賽中，贏得第
一名。
with 有很多意思，在此指「有」（= *having*）。【詳見「文
法寶典」p.607】

49. **C**　除非多找到一些錢，否則戲院就要關門了。
及物動詞非人做主詞要用被動。表「時間」和「條件」的
副詞子句，要用現在式代替未來式，unless「除非」表否
定條件。

50. **A**　The village ***where*** *I was born* has grown into a town.
我出生的那個村莊已經變成一個鎮了。
指定者用定冠詞 the，不指定者用不定冠詞 a。

TEST 8

1. A smile costs _____, but makes people happy.

   A. anything   B. something

   C. nothing   D. everything   【2014 年重慶】

2. During his stay in Xián, Jerry tried almost all the local foods his friends _____.

   A. should recommend

   B. had recommended   C. have recommended

   D. are recommending   【2014 年陝西】

3. You'd better write down her phone number before you _____ it.

   A. forget   B. are forgetting

   C. forgot   D. will forget   【2014 年重慶】

4. The manufacturer comes regularly to collect the cameras _____ to our shop for quality problems.

   A. returning   B. returned

   C. to return

   D. to be returned   【2014 年重慶】

5. I can't tell you _____ way to the Wilsons' because we don't have _____ Wilson here in the village.

   A. the ; a   B. a ; /

   C. a ; the   D. the ; /   【2014 年重慶】

6. She drove so fast through the turn that the car almost went _____ the road.
   A. on
   B. along
   C. from
   D. off   【2014年重慶】

7. James has just arrived, but I didn't know he _____ until yesterday.
   A. will come
   B. was coming
   C. had come
   D. came   【2014年重慶】

8. — Is it true that Mike refused an offer from Yale University yesterday?
   — Yeah, but I have no idea _____ he did it; that's one of his favorite universities.
   A. when
   B. why
   C. that
   D. how   【2014年重慶】

9. Half an hour later, Lucy still couldn't get a taxi _____ the bus had dropped her.
   A. until
   B. when
   C. although
   D. where   【2014年重慶】

10. She'd lived in London and Manchester, but she liked _____ and moved to Cambridge.
    A. both
    B. neither
    C. none
    D. either   【2014年四川】

11. Grandma pointed to the hospital and said, "That's
   _____ I was born."
   A. when   B. how
   C. why   D. where   【2014 年四川】

12. I still remember my happy childhood when my mother
   _____ take me to Disneyland on weekends.
   A. might   B. must
   C. would   D. should   【2014 年四川】

13. I'll be out for some time. _____ anything important
   happens, call me immediately.
   A. In case   B. As if
   C. Even though   D. Now that   【2014 年四川】

14. _____ carefully if any change occurs when doing
   experiments in the lab.
   A. Observe   B. To observe
   C. Observed   D. Observing   【2014 年北京】

15. I borrowed the book *Sherlock Holmes* from the library
   last week, _____ my classmates had recommended
   to me.
   A. who   B. which
   C. when   D. where   【2014 年北京】

16. Writing out all the invitations by hand was more time-consuming than we _____.
    A. will expect   B. are expecting
    C. expect   D. had expected   【2014年山東】

17. I don't really like the author, _____ I have to admit his books are exciting.
    A. although   B. unless
    C. until   D. once   【2014年山東】

18. There's a note pinned to the door _____ when the shop will open again.
    A. saying   B. says
    C. said   D. having said   【2014年山東】

19. It is difficult for us to imagine _____ life was like for slaves in the ancient world.
    A. where   B. what
    C. which   D. why   【2014年山東】

20. The paper is due next month, and I am working seven days _____ week, often long into _____ night.
    A. a ; the   B. the ; 不填
    C. a ; a   D. 不填 ; the   【2014年浙江】

21. An average of just 18.75 cm of rain fell last year, making _____ the driest year since California became a state in 1850.
    A. each   B. it
    C. this   D. one   【2014 年浙江】

22. "Every time you eat a sweet, drink green tea." This is _____ my mother used to tell me.
    A. what   B. how
    C. that   D. whether   【2014 年浙江】

23. Sofia looked around at all the faces: she had the impression that she _____ most of the guests before.
    A. has seen   B. had seen
    C. saw   D. would see   【2014 年浙江】

24. I didn't become a serious climber until the fifth grade, _____ I went up to rescue a kite that was stuck in the branches of a tree.
    A. when   B. where
    C. which   D. why   【2014 年浙江】

25. While staying in the village, James unselfishly shared whatever he had with the villagers without asking for anything _____.
    A. in return   B. in common
    C. in turn   D. in place   【2014 年浙江】

26. Facing up to your problems _____ running away
    from them is the best approach to working things out.
    A. more than   B. rather than
    C. along with   D. or rather   【2014 年浙江】

27. Cathy had quit her job when her son was born _____
    she could stay home and raise her family.
    A. now that   B. as if
    C. only if   D. so that   【2014 年浙江】

28. People won't pay attention to you when they still have
    a lot of ideas of their own crying _____ expression.
    A. from   B. over
    C. with   D. for   【2014 年浙江】

29. Amie Salmon, disabled, is attended throughout her
    school days by a nurse _____ to help her.
    A. to appoint   B. appointing
    C. appointed
    D. having appointed   【2014 年浙江】

30. They were abroad during the months when we were
    carrying out the investigation, or they _____ to our
    help.
    A. would have come   B. could come
    C. have come   D. had come   【2014 年浙江】

31. There is no reason to be disappointed. _____, this could be rather amusing.
    A. Above all   B. As a result
    C. In addition
    D. As a matter of fact   【2014 年浙江】

32. How could you _____ such a fantastic job when you have been out of work for months?
    A. turn off   B. turn in
    C. turn down   D. turn to   【2014 年浙江】

33. _____ the past year as an exchange student in Hong Kong, Linda appears more mature than others of her age.
    A. Spending   B. Spent
    C. Having spent   D. To spend   【2014 年福建】

34. It was culture rather than the language _____ made it hard for him to adapt to the new environment abroad.
    A. where   B. why
    C. that   D. what   【2014 年福建】

35. For those with family members far away, the personal computer and the phone are important in staying

    _____.

    A. connected   B. connecting
    C. to connect   D. to be connected 【2014 年福建】

36. Students should involve themselves in community activities _____ they can gain experience for growth.
    A. who
    B. when
    C. which
    D. where 【2014年福建】

37. _____ no modern communications, we would have to wait for weeks to get news from around the world.
    A. Were there
    B. Had there been
    C. If there are
    D. If there had been 【2014年福建】

38. As a grassroots singer, she reads everything she can _____ concerning music, and takes every opportunity to improve herself.
    A. catch sight of
    B. get hold of
    C. take charge of
    D. make mention of 【2014年福建】

39. — I'm sorry for breaking the cup.
    — Oh, _____ — I've got plenty.
    A. forget it
    B. my pleasure
    C. help yourself
    D. pardon me 【2014年全國大綱】

40. — Is Anne coming tomorrow?
    — _____. If she were to come, she would have called me.
    A. Go ahead
    B. Certainly
    C. That's right
    D. I don't think so 【2014年全國大綱】

41. — I am going to Spain for a holiday soon.

    — _____.

    A. It's my pleasure   B. Never mind

    C. Leave it alone   D. Good for you   【2014 年浙江】

42. — I'd like a wake-up call at 7:00 a.m., please.

    — OK, _____.

    A. help yourself   B. you'll certainly make it

    C. just do what you like

    D. I'll make sure you get one   【2014 年浙江】

43. — I can't remember those grammar rules!

    — _____. I know exactly how you feel.

    A. You're not alone   B. It's hard to say

    C. I'm afraid not   D. It's up to you   【2014 年福建】

44. — Reading is the best way to pass time on the train.

    — _____. I never go traveling without a book.

    A. You are joking   B. That's true

    C. I don't think so   D. It sounds like fun   【2014 年安徽】

45. — I get at least half an hour of exercise almost every day.

    — Oh, great! _____.

    A. Good luck   B. Cheer up

    C. Same to you   D. Keep it up   【2014 年安徽】

46. —— Could I use this dictionary?

—— _____. It's a spare one.

A. Good idea   B. Go ahead

C. You're welcome   D. You'd better not   【2014 年江西】

47. —— Ok, I'll fix your computer right now.

—— Oh, take your time. _____.

A. I can't stand it   B. I'm in no hurry

C. That's a great idea

D. It's not my cup of tea   【2014 年天津】

48. —— How long have you been learning English?

—— About four months.

—— _____! Your English is so good.

A. You can't be serious

B. You got it   C. I couldn't agree more

D. I'm stuck   【2014 年天津】

49. —— I got that job I wanted at the public library.

—— _____! That's good news.

A. Go ahead   B. Cheers

C. Congratulations   D. Come on   【2014 年陝西】

50. —— You know, I met my girlfriend's parents for the first time only yesterday.

—— _____? I thought you'd met them before.

A. So what   B. Pardon

C. Really   D. What for   【2014 年陝西】

Test 8 詳解

1. **C** 微笑不花一毛錢，但是效果很大。

依句意，選 (C) *nothing*。

2. **B** 在傑瑞待在西安時，他嚐過他朋友推薦的所有當地食物。

過去的過去，用「過去完成式」，選 (B) *had recommended*。

3. **A** 在你忘掉以前，最好把她的電話號碼寫下來。

表時間的副詞子句，不能用 shall 或 will 表示未來，要
用現在式代替未來式。

4. **B** 製造商會定期來我們的店裡收那些因為品質有問題而被退還的
相機。

… the cameras *returned to our shop for quality problems.*
源自：… the cameras *which are* returned to our shop
for quality problems.
現在分詞表「主動」，過去分詞表「被動」。
原題用 The producer，改成 The manufacturer 較佳。

5. **A** 我無法告訴你到威爾森家的路，因為村裡沒有人姓威爾森。

the Wilsons' = the Wilsons' house

the way *to the Wilsons'*，有指定，用 the。
專有名詞原則上不加冠詞，但專有名詞普通化時，要加不
定冠詞 a，如 A Miss Chen came to see you this morning.
（今天早上有位陳小姐來看你。）【詳見「文法寶典」p.60】

6. **D** She drove *so* fast *through the turn **that** the car almost*

went <u>off</u> the road.

她經過轉彎處開得非常快，以致於車子幾乎<u>離開</u>道路。

go off the road　離開道路

原題是 at the turn，開車經過，應用 through the turn。

靜態的，才用 at the turn，如：He lost control of the

car at the turn. (他在轉彎處車子失去控制。)

7. **B** ... I didn't know he was coming *until yesterday.*

詹姆士剛剛到達，但我直到昨天才知道他<u>要來</u>。

來去動詞用現在進行式代替未來，配合主要動詞為過去

式，故用過去進行式 was coming。

not…until　直到～才…

8. **B** ── 麥可昨天拒絕耶魯大學提供的入學機會，是真的嗎？

　　── 是啊，但是我不知道他<u>為什麼</u>這樣做；那是他最喜歡的大學

　　　之一。

I have no idea「我不知道」(= *I don't know*)，後可接

名詞子句，依句意，選 (B) ***why***。

9. **D** ... Lucy still couldn't get a taxi ***where** the bus had*

dropped her.

半小時之後，露西仍然沒辦法<u>在下公車的地方</u>找到計程車。

依句意，選 (D) ***where*** 引導的子句才合理。

drop 的主意思是「使掉落」，在這裡是指「讓 (某人) 下車」。

10. **B** 她一直住在倫敦和曼徹斯特，但她<u>兩個都不</u>喜歡，所以就搬到劍橋。

「兩者皆不」，用 *neither*。

11. **D** 祖母指著那家醫院，說：「那就是我出<u>生的地方</u>」。

That's <u>where</u> I was born. 源自 That's *the place* where I was born.

12. **C** I *still* remember my happy childhood *when my mother would*....

我仍然記得我快樂的童年，當時我的母親常在週末帶我去迪士尼。

would 可表「過去的習慣」、「習性、傾向」。【詳見「文法寶典」p.309】

13. **A** ... *In case anything important happens*, call me immediately.

我要出門一段時間。<u>如果</u>有什麼重要的事情發生，立刻打電話給我。

依句意，用 (A) *In case*「如果」(= *If*)。而 (B) As if「好像」，(C) Even though「即使」，(D) Now that「既然」，皆不合句意。

14. **A** <u>Observe</u> *carefully* [*if any change occurs when doing experiments in the lab.*]

要小心<u>觀察</u>在實驗室做實驗時，是否有發生任何變化。

這句話是命令句，要用原形動詞，選 (A) ***Observe*** 「觀察」。

<u>ob</u>¦<u>serve</u>「眼睛不停地看」，引申為：①觀察②遵守。
eye¦ keep

15. **B** 我上星期從圖書館借了《福爾摩斯》，這本書是我同學推薦給
我的。

which 引導形容詞子句，修飾 the book，在子句中做
recommended 的受詞。

Sherlock Holmes〔ˈʃɚlɑkˌhomz〕*n.* 福爾摩斯
recommend *sth.* ***to*** *sb.* 向某人推薦某物

16. **D** Writing out all the invitations *by hand* was more

time-consuming ***than*** we <u>had expected</u>.

用手寫所有的邀請函，比我們預期的還要花時間。

as 和 than 後的 what 可省略。【詳見「文法寶典」p.159】
過去的過去，用「過去完成式」。　　***write out*** 寫出

17. **A** 我不是真的很喜歡那個作者，但是我必須承認他的書很精彩刺激。
依句意，選 (A) ***although***。
although 可以指「雖然；然而；但是」，在此作「但是」解。

18. **A** 門上釘著一張紙條，上面說這家店何時會重新開張。

There's a note *pinned to the door* <u>saying</u> ***when*** ....

= There's a note pinned to the door *which says* when ....

分詞片語當形容詞用。

note *n.* 紙條　　pin *v.* (用大頭針) 固定

19. **B** It is difficult *for us* to imagine ***what*** life was like

虛主詞　　眞正主詞

for slaves in the ancient world.

我們很難想像，在古代，奴隸是過著什麼樣的生活。

疑問代名詞 what 引導名詞子句，做 imagine 的受詞，
在子句中，what 做介系詞 like 的受詞。

20. **A** 報告下個月要交，我一星期工作七天，常常到深夜。

「一個星期」用 a week，指定的夜晚用 the。

long into the night 到深夜 (= *late into the night*)

21. **B** 去年平均降雨量是 18.75 公分，是自從加州於 1850 年設立以來
最乾燥的一年。

it 代替前面的 last year，其他選項無法代替時間。

22. **A** "***Every time*** you eat a sweet, drink green tea." This is

what my mother used to tell me.

「每次你吃甜食時，就要喝綠茶。」這是我母親以前告訴過
我的。

前面缺一個字，後面缺一個字，用 ***what***。

複合關係代名詞 what，引導名詞子句做 is 的補語，在子
句中，what 做 tell 的直接受詞。

used to + V. 以前

23. **B** 蘇菲亞環顧四周，看所有的面孔；她有印象，以前<u>看過</u>大部份的客人。

過去的過去，用「過去完成式」。

24. **A** 直到五年級，我才成為很認真的攀登者，<u>當時</u>我爬上去解救一個卡在樹枝中的風箏。

依句意，選 (A) *when*。　　*be stuck in* 被卡在…

25. **A** 當詹姆士待在村莊時，他無私地和村民分享他的一切，不要求任何<u>回報</u>。

依句意，選 (A) *in return*「作為回報」。而 (B) in common「共同的」，(C) in turn「結果；後來」，(D) in place「在合適的位置」，則不合句意。

26. **B** Facing up to your problems *rather than running away from them is....*

面對你的問題，<u>而不是</u>逃避問題，是解決事情最好的方法。

依句意，選 (B) *rather than*「而不是」(= *instead of*)。

face up to 面對 (= *face*)

approach 主要的用法是動詞，作「接近」解，在此當名詞，作「方法」解，後面介系詞用 to。

27. **D** Cathy had quit her job *when her son was born **so that** she could stay home and raise her family.*

凱西當她的兒子出生時就把工作辭掉了，<u>以便</u>待在家裡養育小孩。

so that 引導副詞子句，表「目的」，等於 in order that。
family 一般作「家庭；家人」解，在此作「子女；孩子」解。

28. **D** … a lot of ideas *of their own crying for expression.*
當人們仍然有很多自己的想法急於表達時，就不會注意聽你說。
cry for 迫切需要 (= *cry out for*)

29. **C** Amie Salmon, *disabled*, is attended *throughout her*

school days by a nurse *appointed to help her.*
艾咪‧薩蒙因為殘障，就學期間都有一位護士被指定來幫助她。

disabled「殘障的」是插入語，throughout her school
days 是介詞片語，做副詞用，修飾 attended，句中 be
attended by 指「被～照顧」，a nurse ***appointed*** to
help her 源自 a nurse ***who is appointed*** to help her。
attend 主要意思是「參加；出席」，在此指「照顧；照料」
(= *look after*)。
原題是 guard her「看守她」，改成 help her 較合理。

30. **A** They were abroad *during the months **when** we were*

carrying out the investigation, ***or*** they would have

come to our help.
在我們執行調查那幾個月，他們都在國外，否則，他們就會來
幫助我們。

前面是直說法的過去式，敘述事實，後面是假設法，與
過去事實相反，故選選 (A) ***would have come***。

31. **D** 沒有理由失望。<u>事實上</u>，這可能很有趣。

依句意，選 (D)。在此 could 表輕微的懷疑。【詳見「文法寶典」p.315】

> *as a matter of fac*t　事實上
> = in fact
> = in effect
> = in truth
> = in reality
> = in actuality

【詳見「一口氣背同義字寫作文」p.225「寫作文必備轉承語」】
做文法題目，無形中也學會寫作文。

32. **C** 這個時候你已經失業了幾個月，你怎麼可以<u>拒絕</u>這麼棒的工作呢？

turn down 有二個主要意思：①拒絕②調小（聲、寬度等）
此處的 could 表客氣。【詳見「文法寶典」p.314】

33. **C** 過去一年在香港當交換學生，琳達現在看起來比同年齡的學生
成熟。

Having spent the past year…, Linda appears….
= *As she has spent* the past year…, Linda appears….
完成式分詞構句表比主要動詞早完成。【詳見「文法寶典」p.461】

34. **C** 是文化而不是語言，讓他很難適應國外的新環境。

It was … that 爲強調句型，只要將這三字去掉，就恢復
原句。

… made *it* hard *for him to adapt to*….

rather than 而不是（= *instead of*）

35. A 對那些有家人在遠方的人，個人電腦和電話對保持<u>聯繫</u>很重要。

stay，*go*，*come*，*sit* 等後面常接**分詞**或**形容詞**，做主詞補語，根據句意，人們「被連接」在一起，應用過去分詞，表被動。

36. D 學生應當參與能夠讓他們得到成長經驗的社區活動。

… activites *where* they can gain experience of growth.

where 引導形容詞子句，修飾 activities，子句爲完整句，不可用關代 which。

involve 原來的意思是「捲入」，involve oneself in（把自己捲入）引申爲「參與」（= *be involved in*）。

37. A 如果沒有現代的通訊系統，我們就必須等幾個禮拜，才能得到來自全世界的新聞。

Were there no modern communications, ….

= *If there were* no modern communications, ….

communications *n.* 通訊；通訊系統（= *a system for sending in formation*）

… we would have to wait *for weeks* to get news *from around the world*.

介詞片語做介詞的受詞，情況很少，可把 from around，from behind，from under 等看成「雙重介系詞」。【詳見「文法寶典」p.545】

38. **B** … she reads everything *she can get hold of concerning music,* ….

身為草根歌手，她儘量閱讀她所能得到有關音樂的一切，並且把握每次機會，改善她自己。

> *get hold of* 抓住
> = take hold of
> = catch hold of
> = catch

grassroots singer 草根歌手【歌唱內容有關一般人的問題】

39. **A** — 抱歉把杯子打破了。

— 噢，別放在心上 — 我有很多個。

對於 I'm sorry. 的回答，可用 Forget it. 或 Forget about it.

其他答案用在：

> A : Thanks for the help.
> B : *My pleasure*. 我的榮幸。

> A : Do you have anything to drink?
> B : *Help yourself*. 請自己拿。

> A : Sorry, that seat is taken. 抱歉，那個位子有人坐。
> B : Pardon me. 抱歉。

40. **D** — 安妮明天會來嗎？

— 我覺得不會。如果她要來，她會打電話給我。

依句意，選 (D) I *don't think so*.

If 子句是假設法未來式，主要子句是假設法過去式。
If 子句和主要子句的時態不一定一致。

41. **D** — 我不久就要去西班牙度假。

— <u>你真行</u>。

> ***Good for you***. 源自 *It is* good for you.，字面意思是「對你很好。」引申為「你真行；你真棒；你做得太好了；你真厲害」，這句話美國人常用，當你看到同學考高分，你就可以說：*Good for you*. (你真行。) 當你看到別人買了新電腦，你也可以說：*Good for you*. (你真厲害。) 凡是別人有消息，你都可以說：*Good for you*. 在本題中，聽到別人要去旅行，除了 "Good for you." 以外，美國人還常說：*Have a nice trip*. (祝你旅途愉快。) 或 *Enjoy yourself*. (好好玩。)

42. **D** — 請給我早上七點鐘的叫醒電話。

— 好，<u>我確定你會接到</u>。

依句意，選 (D) *I'll make sure you get one*.

43. **A** — 我記不住那些文法規則。

— <u>不只你有這個問題</u>。我完全知道你的感覺。

> ***You are not alone***. 字面意思是「你並不孤單。」引申為「不只你有這個問題。」或「很多人都有這個問題。」
> (= *Many people have that problem*.)
> 原題是 Practice more. (多練習。) 改成：I know exactly how you feel. 較佳。

44. **B** ── 閱讀是在火車上消磨時間最好的方法。

── 你說得對。我旅行一定帶本書。

> ***That's true.*** 你說得對。
> = That's the truth. 那是事實。
> = That's so true. 你說得很對。
> = That's really true. 你說得真對。

當贊同別人的時候，你可以連續說九句：

> I agree. 我同意。
> I'm with you. 我支持你。
> You're absolutely right. 你說得完全對。
>
> That's for sure. 那是確定的。
> That's the truth. 那是事實。
> That's how I feel. 我也有同樣的感覺。
>
> I feel the same way. 我有同感。
> I couldn't agree more. 我完全同意。
> You're right on the money. 你說得非常正確。

【詳見「一口氣背會話」p.588】

45. **D** 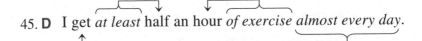 I get *at least* half an hour *of exercise almost every day*.

── 我幾乎每天至少做半小時的運動。

── 噢，太好了。繼續做。

keep up 和 keep it up 不一樣，keep up 作「跟上」解。

【詳見「一口氣背會話」p.684】

46. **B** — 我可以用這本字典嗎？

— <u>拿去用吧</u>。這本是多的。

這裡回答除了用 "Go ahead." 以外，還可以用 "Sure."
（當然可以。）或 "No problem."（沒問題。）
It's a spare one. 意思是「這本是多的。」（ = *It's an extra
one.*）表示「我可能有兩本。」

47. **B** — 好，我馬上來修你的電腦。

— 噢，慢慢來。<u>我不急</u>。

> ***I'm in no hurry.*** 我不急。
> = I'm not in a hurry. 我不急。
> = I'm not pressed for time. 我不趕時間。
> = I can wait. 我可以等。
> 【詳見「一口氣背會話」p.380】

> right now 馬上；立刻
> = right away
> = at once
> = immediately

48. **A** — 你學英文多久了？

— 大約四個月。

— <u>你不是當真的吧！</u>你的英文這麼好。

You can't be serious. 你不是當真的吧。
= You must be joking. 你一定在開玩笑。

serious 主要意思是「認真的；嚴肅的」，在此作「當真
的；不開玩笑的」。

B. You got it.　你懂了。

C. I couldn't agree more.　我完全同意。

D. I'm stuck.　我不知道該怎麼辦。（= *I don't know what to do.*）

49. **C** — I got that job *I wanted at the public library.*

我得到市立圖書館我想要的工作了。

— 恭喜恭喜！那眞是好消息。

> 下列名詞要用複數形：
> congratulations（恭喜），greetings（問候），
> regards（問候），wishes（祝福），
> surroundings（環境），circumstances（環境），
> riches（財富），savings（存款），thanks（感謝）等。
> 【詳見「文法寶典」p.84】

50. **C** — I met my girlfriend's parents *for the first time*

only yesterday.

我只有在昨天才第一次見到我女朋友的父母親。

— 眞的嗎？我以爲你之前就見過他們了。

only 是副詞，加強 yesterday 的語氣，等於 just，句中不用 only 也可以。

TEST 9

1. — Is Peter coming?

   — No, he _____ his mind at the last minute after a
   phone call.

   A. changes   B. changed

   C. was changing   D. had changed   【2015 年重慶】

2. The meeting will be held in September, but _____
   knows the date for sure.

   A. everybody   B. nobody

   C. anybody   D. somebody   【2015 年重慶】

3. If you miss this chance, it may be years _____ you
   get another one.

   A. as   B. before

   C. since   D. after   【2015 年重慶】

4. We must find out _____ Karl is coming so that we
   can book a room for him.

   A. when   B. how

   C. where   D. why   【2015 年重慶】

5. — Hello Jenny, can I see Ms. Lewis?

   — _____. I'll tell her you're here.

   A. With pleasure   B. Never mind

   C. You're welcome   D. Just a minute 【2015 年重慶】

6. _____ the early flight, we ordered a taxi in advance and got up very early.

    A. Catching   B. Caught

    C. To catch   D. Catch   【2015 年北京】

7. — Did you enjoy the party?

    — Yes, we _____ well by our hosts.

    A. were treated   B. would be treated

    C. treated   D. had treated   【2015 年北京】

8. The park was full of people _____ themselves in the sunshine.

    A. having enjoyed   B. enjoyed

    C. enjoying   D. to enjoy   【2015 年北京】

9. Opposite is St. Paul's Church, _____ you can hear some lovely music.

    A. which   B. that

    C. when   D. where   【2015 年北京】

10. He is a shy man, _____ he is not afraid of anything or anyone.

    A. so   B. but

    C. or   D. as   【2015 年北京】

11. In the last few years, China _____ great things in environmental protection.
    A. has achieved   B. was achieved
    C. was achieving   D. is achieving   【2015 年北京】

12. — Did you have difficulty finding Ann's house?
    — Not really. She _____ us clear directions and we were able to find it easily.
    A. was to give   B. had given
    C. was giving   D. would give   【2015 年北京】

13. You won't find paper cutting difficult _____ you keep practicing it.
    A. even though   B. as long as
    C. as if   D. ever since   【2015 年北京】

14. — Can't you stay a little longer?
    — It's getting late. I really _____ go now. My daughter is home alone.
    A. may   B. can
    C. must   D. dare   【2015 年北京】

15. — Dr. Jackson is not in his office at the moment.
    — All right. I _____ him later.
    A. will call   B. have called
    C. call   D. will be calling   【2015 年北京】

16. If _____ for the job, you'll be informed soon.

    A. to select   B. select

    C. selecting   D. selected   【2015 年北京】

17. I truly believe _____ beauty comes from within.

    A. that   B. where

    C. what   D. why   【2015 年北京】

18. If I _____ it with my own eyes, I wouldn't have believed it.

    A. didn't see

    B. weren't seeing

    C. wouldn't see

    D. hadn't seen   【2015 年北京】

19. Last year was the warmest year on record, with global temperatures 0.68 °C _____ average.

    A. below   B. on

    C. at   D. above   【2015 年重慶】

20. The number of smokers, _____ reported, has dropped by 17 percent in just one year.

    A. it   B. which

    C. what   D. as   【2015 年江蘇】

21. _____ much time sitting at a desk, office workers are generally troubled by health problems.
    A. Being spent   B. Having spent
    C. Spent   D. Spending   【2015 年江蘇】

22. It is so cold that you can't go outside _____ fully covered in thick clothes.
    A. if   B. unless
    C. once   D. when   【2015 年江蘇】

23. The university started some new language programs to _____ the country's Silk Road Economic Belt.
    A. apply to   B. cater to
    C. appeal to   D. hunt for   【2015 年江蘇】

24. It might have saved me some trouble _____ the schedule.
    A. did I know   B. have I known
    C. do I know   D. had I known   【2015 年江蘇】

25. — Why didn't you invite John to your birthday party?
    — Well, you know he's _____.
    A. an early bird
    B. a wet blanket
    C. a lucky dog
    D. a tough nut   【2015 年江蘇】

26. — Sorry, Liz. I think I was a bit rude to you.

— _____, but don't do that again!

A. Go ahead   B. Forget it

C. It depends   D. With pleasure   【2015 年江蘇】

27. Only when Lily walked into the office _____ that she had left the contract at home.

A. she realized

B. has she realized

C. she has realized

D. did she realize   【2015 年天津】

28. — Jack, you seem excited.

— _____! I won the first prize.

A. Guess what   B. So what

C. Pardon me   D. Who cares   【2015 年天津】

29. _____ in painting, John didn't notice evening approaching.

A. To absorb   B. To be absorbed

C. Absorbed   D. Absorbing   【2015 年天津】

30. Jane can't attend the meeting at 3 o'clock this afternoon because she _____ a class at that time.

A. will teach   B. would teach

C. has taught   D. will be teaching   【2015 年天津】

31. I _____ have worried before I came to my new
    school, for my classmates here are very friendly to me.
    A. mightn't   B. mustn't
    C. needn't   D. couldn't   【2015 年天津】

32. _____ for two days, Steve managed to finish his
    report on schedule.
    A. To work   B. Worked
    C. To be working   D. Having worked   【2015 年天津】

33. Despite the previous rounds of talks, no agreement
    _____ so far by the two sides.
    A. has been reached
    B. was reached
    C. will reach
    D. will have reached   【2015 年天津】

34. We need to get to the root of the problem _____ we
    can solve it.
    A. while   B. after
    C. before   D. as   【2015 年天津】

35. I wish I _____ at my sister's wedding last Tuesday,
    but I was on a business trip in New York then.
    A. will be   B. would be
    C. have been   D. had been   【2015 年天津】

36. See, your computer has broken down again! It doesn't
   _____ sense to buy the cheapest brand of computer
   just to save a few dollars.
   A. have   B. make
   C. display   D. bring   【2015 年天津】

37. The boss of the company is trying to create an easy
   atmosphere _____ his employees enjoy their work.
   A. where   B. which
   C. when   D. who   【2015 年天津】

38. — Can you come to a party on Saturday, Peter?
   — Oh, _____ I'm already going out, I'm afraid.
   A. what a pity!   B. don't ask!
   C. how come?   D. so what?   【2015 年安徽】

39. Just as I got to the school gate, I realized I _____ my
   bag in the café.
   A. have left   B. had left
   C. would leave   D. was leaving   【2015 年安徽】

40. It is reported that a space station _____ on the moon
   in years to come.
   A. will be building   B. will be built
   C. has been building
   D. has been built   【2015 年安徽】

41. It was so noisy that we _____ hear ourselves think.

    A. couldn't   B. shouldn't

    C. mustn't   D. needn't   【2015 年浙江】

42. Listening to music at home is one thing, hearing it
    _____ live is quite another.

    A. perform   B. performing

    C. to perform   D. performed   【2015 年浙江】

43. Creating an atmosphere _____ employees feel part
of a team is a big challenge.

    A. as   B. whose

    C. in which   D. at which   【2015 年浙江】

44. — Sorry, I forgot to lock the door.

    — _____. Mike can do it later.

    A. No way

    B. Take your time

    C. No problem

    D. You're welcome   【2015 年四川】

45. You _____ be careful with the camera. It cost a lot!

    A. must   B. may

    C. can   D. will   【2015 年四川】

46. The books on the desk, _____ covers are shiny, are prizes for us.
    A. which
    B. what
    C. whose
    D. that 【2015 年四川】

47. More expressways _____ in Sichuan soon to promote the local economy.
    A. are being built
    B. will be built
    C. have been built
    D. had been built 【2015 年四川】

48. There is only one more day to go _____ your favorite music group plays live.
    A. since
    B. until
    C. when
    D. before 【2015 年四川】

49. Little Tom sat _____ watching the monkey dancing in front of him.
    A. amaze
    B. amazing
    C. amazed
    D. to amaze 【2015 年四川】

50. Niki is always full of ideas, but _____ is useful to my knowledge.
    A. neither
    B. no one
    C. another
    D. none 【2015 年四川】

Test 9 詳解

1. **B** —— 彼得要來嗎？

—— 不，他在最後一分鐘接到一通電話，他就改變主意了。

No, he <u>changed</u> his mind *at the last minute after a phone call*.

依句意，該用「過去式」。

2. **B** The meeting will be held *in September*, but ***nobody***

knows the date *for sure*.

會議將在九月舉行，但是沒人確實知道日期。

依句意，選 (B) ***nobody***。

3. **B** ***If you miss this chance***, it may be years ***before*** you get

another one.

如果你錯過這次機會，可能要好幾年，你才會有另一個機會。

years 在此等於 many years（很多年）或 several years

（好幾年）。

4. **A** We must find out ***when Karl is coming so that*** we can

名 詞 子 句

book a room for him.

我們必須查出卡爾<u>什麼時候</u>來，以便我們可以爲他預訂一個房間。

find out 發現；查明；弄清楚

so that 引導表「目的」的副詞子句，修飾 find，原試題中用 so，是中文思想，中文的「所以」可表「目的」和「結果」，但英文中，so 只表「結果」。

5. **D** — Hello. Jenny, can I see Ms. Lewis?

— <u>Just a minute</u>. I'll tell her you're here.

— 哈囉，珍妮，我可以見劉易士女士嗎？

— <u>請稍等</u>。我會告訴她你在這裡。

Ms.〔mɪz〕*n.* 女士；小姐【未婚、已婚皆可用】

Lewis〔'ljuɪs〕*n.* 劉易士

> ***Just a minute****.* 請稍等。(源自 Please wait ***just a minute****.*)
> = ***Just a moment****.*
> = ***Just a second****.*

6. **C** <u>*To catch* the early flight</u>, we ordered a taxi *in advance and* got up *very early*.

<u>爲了要趕</u>早班飛機，我們事先預約了計程車，很早就起床。

To catch = In order to catch，不定詞表「目的」，但在此不用較好，避免和後面的 ordered 重覆。分詞構句可以表「原因」、「時間」、「條件」、「讓步」、「附帶狀態」，但不可表「目的」。

7. **A** — Did you enjoy the party?

— Yes, we <u>were treated</u> *well by our hosts.*

— 你喜歡這個派對嗎?

— 是的,我們受到主人很好的<u>招待</u>。

這條題目考時態和被動,依句意要用過去式被動,句中 hosts 用複數,表示主人不只一位,即使是「女主人」,也用 host,現在 hostess 多指「女服務員」,叫 waitress 較不禮貌,就像現在酒店、夜總會裡,男生叫「少爺」,女生叫「公主」。

8. **C** The park was full of people *enjoying themselves in the sunshine.*

公園裡擠滿了人,他們在陽光下<u>玩得很愉快</u>。

enjoying 源自 who were enjoying,enjoy 是及物動詞,接反身代名詞做受詞。

> *enjoy* oneself 玩得愉快 　　in the sunshine　在陽光下
> = *have a good time*　　 = in the sun
> = *have fun*

9. **D** Opposite is St. Paul's Church, ***where*** *you can hear some lovely music.*

對面是聖保羅教堂,<u>在那裡</u>你可以聽到美妙的音樂。

依句意選 (D) where,引導形容詞子句,修飾 Church。which 是關代,該有代名作用才對。

St. 源自 saint，唸成〔sent〕，是「聖人」之意。

St. Paul〔sent'pol〕*n.* 聖保羅

這句話是倒裝句，本來是 St. Paul's Church is opposite，因為主詞後有很長的修飾語，為避免頭重腳輕而倒裝。

【詳見「文法寶典」p.636】補語放在句尾的倒裝，又如：

Happy is he *who has a sound mind in a sound body.*
（身心健全的人才是幸福的。）

  opposite *adj.* 在對面的
= on the other side of the road

10. **B** 他是個害羞的人，<u>但是</u>他不害怕任何事或任何人。

依句意，選 (B) *but*。

11. **A** *In the last few years*, China <u>has achieved</u> great things

in environmental protection.

在最近幾年來，中國在環境保護方面<u>已經有</u>很大的成就。

last 主要意思是「最後的」，在這裡指「最近的」
（ = *past*「剛剛過去的」）。

原試題用 *has made great achievements*（誤）是中式英文，美國人不用。in 在這裡表「經過」，比 for 語氣弱，在此若用 for，整句要改成：For the last few years, China **has been achieving** great things in environmental protection.（最近幾年來，中國在環境保護方面，<u>一直</u>有很大的成就。）

12. **B** — Did you have difficulty *(in) finding Ann's house?*

— Not really. She <u>had given</u> us clear directions

and we were able to find it *easily.*

— 你找到安的家有困難嗎？

— 並沒有。她<u>給了</u>我們明確的方向，我們能夠輕鬆找到。

> 很多中國人不會用 Not really.，這句話用來表示模糊的
> 回答，如：
> A：Are you busy? 你忙嗎？
> B：*Not really.* 沒有真的忙。
> Not really. 在這裡的意思是「我現在在忙，但我可以替你
> 做事。」(= *I'm doing something, but I have time for you.*)
> 同義片語有：Not exactly. (不完全正確。)
> Not particularly. (沒有特別地。) (= *Not especially.*)
> 本題根據句意，表示「過去已經」，應用「過去完成式」。

13. **B** You won't find paper cutting difficult <u>***as long as***</u> you

keep practicing it.

<u>只要</u>你持續練習，你就不會覺得剪紙很難。

根據句意，表「條件」，用 (B) *as long as* 只要 (= *so long as* = *if*)。

14. **C** — 你不能再待久一點嗎？

— 時間越來越晚了。我現在真的<u>必須</u>走了。我女兒單獨在家。

根據句意，只有 (C) *must*「必須」合理。

15. **A** ── 傑克森博士現在不在辦公室。

　　 ── 好的。我稍後再<u>打電話給</u>他。

　　依句意用「未來式」，選 (A) *will call*。

16. **D** *If* (*you are*) <u>*selected*</u> *for the job*, you'll be informed *soon*.

　　如果你被<u>選上</u>這個工作，我們會很快通知你。

　　If 和 When 引導的副詞子句，句意明確時，可省略主詞和 be 動詞。原試題用 *If accepted for the job*, ... (如果你被接受) 是中式英文。

17. **A** 我眞的相信，美麗來自內心。

　　把 *from within* 當做慣用語來看，作「從內部」解 (= *from inside*)。

18. **D** *If I* <u>*hadn't seen*</u> *it with my own eyes*, I wouldn't have believed it.

　　如果我不是自己親眼<u>看見</u>，我就不會相信。

　　這句話是典型的「假設法過去式」，If 子句用「過去完成式」，表「與過去事實相反」。

19. **D** Last year was the warmest year *on record, with global temperatures* 0.68 °C <u>*above*</u> *average*.

去年是紀錄上最熱的一年，全球溫度<u>高於</u>平均值 0.68 °C。

$$\left.\begin{array}{l}\text{with}\\\text{without}\end{array}\right\} + \text{受} + \text{受補} \quad \text{表「伴隨」}$$

above average 高於平均數（不可寫成 *above the average*）
below average 低於平均數（不可寫成 *below the average*）

20. **D** The number *of smokers*, **<u>as</u>** reported, has dropped *by 17 percent in just one year.*

<u>根據報導</u>，抽煙的人數僅僅只有一年，下降了百分之十七。

as reported 源自 ***as it is reported***，省略了主詞和 be 動詞，典型的例子有：Come as soon ***as possible***.（請儘快趕來。）源自 Come as soon ***as it is possible***.

21. **B** [*Having spent* much time sitting at a desk,] office workers are *generally* troubled *by health problems.*

因為辦公室的員工<u>花</u>很長的時間坐在桌子前面，他們通常都受到健康問題的困擾。

= ***As*** they ***have spent*** much time sitting at a desk, office workers are generally troubled by health problems.

按照句意，應用「分詞構句完成式」，表示比主要動詞先發生，as 在此表「原因」+「時間」。【詳見「文法寶典」p.461】

如選 (D)，句子應改成 ***Spending so*** much time sitting at a desk, office workers are generally troubled by health problems. 此時強調因果關係，分詞構句簡單式

表示和主要動詞時間相同，等於 *As* they spend *so* much time sitting at a desk, office workers....。外國人學英文真的很難，多一個 so 語氣就不一樣了，所以，背短句是最簡單的方法。

22. **B** 天氣太冷了，你不能出去，<u>除非你全身被厚衣服包得滿滿的</u>。

unless (*you are*) fully covered...，unless 後句意明顯，省略主詞和 be 動詞。

23. **B** 這所大學開設了一些新的語言課程，為了<u>迎合</u>國家的絲綢之路經濟帶<u>的需要</u>。

(A) apply to　應用於　　　(B) *cater to*　迎合；滿足需要

(C) appeal to　吸引　　　　(D) hunt for　尋找

24. **D** <u>如果我知道</u>這個行程，就會節省我很多麻煩。

had I known = *if I had known*（假設法過去式）

25. **B** ― 你為什麼不邀請約翰參加你的生日派對？

― 嗯，你知道他是個<u>掃興的人</u>。

(A) an early bird　早起者　　(B) *a wet blanket*　掃興的人

(C) a lucky dog　幸運者　　　(D) a tough nut　難題

26. **B** ― 對不起，麗茲。我想我對妳有一點不禮貌。

― <u>沒關係</u>，但下次不要這麼做了！

(A) 去做吧　　　　　　　　(B) <u>沒關係</u>

(C) 視情況而定　　　　　　(D) 很樂意

對於 I'm sorry. 的回答有：

Forget it.
= Forget about it.
= Forgive and forget.

= Don't worry about it.
= No problem.
= Never mind.

= I forgive you.
= You're forgiven.
= All is forgiven.

= That's all right.
= That's okay.
= It's okay.

【詳見 NTC's Dictionary of EVERYDAY AMERICAN ENGLISH EXPRESSIONS p.153】

27. **D** ***Only when*** *Lily walked into the office* <u>did she realize</u>

<u>***that*** *she had left the contract at home*</u>.
　　　　名詞子句　　　　　　　受補

唯有當莉莉走進辦公室時，她才<u>知道</u>，她把合約留在家裡。

Only +
{
副詞
副詞子句
副詞片語
}
+ 助 V + S + V.

依句意應該用「過去式」，表示過去一點時間，而不是「已經知道」，不能用「完成式」。

28. **A** —— 傑克，你似乎很興奮。

　　—— <u>你猜猜看</u>！我得了頭獎。

這句話也可回答成：You'll never guess.（你絕對猜不
到。）或 You won't believe it.（你不會相信。）

the first prize ①頭獎 ②第一名（= *the first place*）

29. **C** *Absorbed* in painting, John didn't notice evening
approaching.
現分→受補　　　　　　　　　　　　　　感官動詞

因為專心於畫畫，約翰沒有注意到天黑了。

= ***As he was*** absorbed in painting, John....

　　be absorbed in 專心於

如選 (B)，不定詞片語表「目的」，句意不合。

30. **D** Jane can't attend the meeting *at 3 o'clock this afternoon*
[***because*** *she will be teaching a class at that time.*]

珍不能參加今天下午 3 點鐘的會議，因為她那時要教課。

依句意，表示未來某時正在進行的動作，該用「未來進
行式」。

31. **C** I needn't have worried ***before*** *I came to my new school,* ....

我來這所新學校之前不必擔心的，因為這裡的同學都對我非常
友善。

needn't have p.p. 表示「過去不必做而已做」，其他選
項句意不合。

32. **D** *Having worked* for two days, Steve managed to finish

his report *on schedule*.

= *After* he **had worked** for two days, Steve….

工作了二天以後，史蒂夫勉強準時完成他的報告。

完成式的分詞表示比主要動詞先發生。

manage to V. ①設法（= *find a way to*）

②能做到；勉強做到（= *be able to*）

on schedule 按照進度；準時

33. **A** *Despite the previous rounds of talks*, no agreement has

been reached *so far by the two sides*.

儘管先前的幾回合會談，到目前爲止，雙方尚未達成協議。

這條題目是考時態和被動，so far「到目前爲止」，和

「現在完成式」連用。

round〔raʊnd〕*n.* 回合

reach an agreement 達成協議；達成共識

34. **C** We need to get to the root *of the problem **before** we*

can solve it.

在我們能夠解決問題之前，我們必須先找到問題的根源。

get to the root of 找出～的根源

= **get to the bottom of**

依句意選 (C) **before**。

35. **D**　I wish I <u>had been</u> at my sister's wedding *last Tuesday*,
　　but….

　　我希望我上週二<u>有參加</u>我妹妹的婚禮，但是我當時在紐約出差。

　　wish 後用過去完成式，表示過去沒有實現的希望。

36. **B**　你看看，你的電腦又壞了！只是爲了省幾塊錢，去買最便宜的
　　品牌的電腦，實在沒<u>有</u>意義。

　　make sense　有意義；講得通；合情合理

> ***see***　你看看（做插入語）
> = ***you see***
> = ***look***（不能用 *you look*）

37. **A**　… an easy atmosphere ***where*** *his employees enjoy their*

　　work.

　　這家公司的老板想要創造一個員工可以享受工作的輕鬆氣氛。

　　where 引導形容詞子句，修飾 atmosphere，子句中
　　where 無代名作用。(B) ***which*** 有代名作用，文法不合。

38. **A**　── 彼得，星期六你可以來參加派對嗎？

　　── 噢！<u>眞可惜</u>！我恐怕已經出去了。

> ***What a pity!***　眞可惜！
> = ***What a shame!***　眞是遺憾！
> = ***That's too bad.***　眞糟糕。

39. **B**　*Just **as** I got to the school gate*, I realized I <u>had left</u> my

　　bag *in the café*.

就在我到達學校門口的時候，我才知道我把我的包包留在咖啡廳了。

café〔ˋkæˋfe〕*n.* 咖啡廳（= *coffee shop*）

過去的過去，用「過去完成式」。

Just as 就在…時；正當

= ***Just when***

40. **B** ***It*** is reported [***that*** a space station <u>will be built</u> *on the moon in years to come.*]

根據報導，在未來幾年，就會在月球上<u>建立</u>太空站。

> ***in years to come*** 在未來幾年
> = ***in the coming years***
> = ***in the future*** 在未來

41. **A** It was *so* noisy ***that*** we <u>couldn't</u> hear ourselves think.

這裡眞的是太吵了。

根據句意選 (A) ***couldn't***。

原題是 We couldn't hear ourselves speak. 字典上查不到，問了所有的外國人都沒聽過，所以把 speak 改成 think。I couldn't hear myself think. 是一個慣用語，表示「太吵了。」（= *There is too much noise.*）

42. **D** Listening *to music at home* is ***one thing***, hearing it

<u>performed</u> *live* is *quite **another***.

在家聽音樂是一回事，聽現場表演又是另一回事。

這條題目考感官動詞，「hear + 受詞 + 過去分詞」表「被動」。原題是 … going to hear it being performed live… 是中式英文。

perform live 現場表演，live〔laɪv〕是副詞，作「現場」解。

43. **C** Creating an atmosphere ***in which*** *employees feel part of*
　　　　　　　　　　　　　　　　　　where
　　a team is a big challenge.

創造一個員工感到是團隊一分子的氣氛，是一大挑戰。

「介詞 + 關代」等於關副，which 代替 atmosphere，只能說 ***in*** an atmosphere，不能說 ***at*** an atmosphere（誤），故本題選 (C) ***in which***。

44. **C** — 抱歉，我忘了鎖門。

　　　　— 沒問題。麥克待會可以去鎖。

(A) 不行　　　(B) 慢慢來　　　(C) 沒問題　　　(D) 不客氣

【請參閱第 26 題 p.19】

45. **A** 你必須小心使用照相機。它值很多錢！

　　　　依句意選 (A) ***must***。

46. **C** The books *on the desk*, ***whose*** *covers are shiny*, are

　　prizes *for us*.

書桌上的書是給我們的獎品，書的封面很閃亮。

shiny〔ˈʃaɪnɪ〕*adj.* 發亮的；閃亮的

依句意，選所有格關代 whose，引導形容詞子句，修飾 books。

47. **B** 四川很快就要興建更多高速公路，以提升當地的經濟。

本題考時態，表未來用「未來式」，依句意用被動 *will be built*。

48. **B** There is *only* one *more* day *to go* <u>***until***</u> *your favorite music group plays live.*

<u>距離</u>你最喜歡的音樂團體現場演出只剩一天了。

前有比較級形容詞或副詞時，常用 until 代替 before。

not…until 直到…才　　　*more…until* 還有…才

【比較】 It's more than two hours *until* your train leaves.

（距離你的火車開車還有二個多小時。）

It will be two hours *before* your train leaves.

（還有二小時你的火車就要開了。）

49. **C** 小湯姆坐在那裡<u>很吃驚</u>，看到猴子在他前面跳舞。

$$S + \begin{cases} \text{sit} \\ \text{stand} \\ \text{come} \\ \text{go} \\ \text{keep} \\ \text{remain} \end{cases} + 分詞（分詞做主詞補語，amaze「使吃驚」是情感動詞，修飾人須用過去分詞）$$

50. **D** 妮基總是有很多點子，但據我所知，<u>沒有一個</u>有用。

依句意選 (D) *none*，none 用於人或物均可，而 no one 僅用於人（＝*nobody*）。

TEST 10

1. I will forgive him _____ he tells the truth.
   A. unless   B. so
   C. even though   D. as long as   【建中 1】

2. It's been two years _____ Jimmy.
   A. that I don't see
   B. that I haven't seen
   C. since I last saw
   D. since I see   【北一女 1】

3. The book _____ fifty dollars.
   A. pays   B. spends
   C. costs   D. sells   【中和高中 1】

4. I hope Bus 33 comes soon. I _____ for 30 minutes.
   A. am waited   B. have been waiting
   C. waited   D. waiting   【中和高中 1】

5. He owed his success _____ his parents and his teachers.
   A. to   B. for
   C. as   D. with   【中和高中 1】

6. I'll go to the basketball game _____ I have an
   important exam tomorrow.
   A. I bet   B. for sure
   C. it seems   D. even if   【華江高中 1】

7. Cindy has been working here _____.
   A. for six months
   B. since six months
   C. six months ago
   D. six months   【北一女 1】

8. His actions didn't agree _____ his words.
   A. with   B. to
   C. as   D. about   【建中 1】

9. Hurry up, _____ we will miss the opening of the
   movie.
   A. and   B. but
   C. or   D. for   【建中 1】

10. What you told me is true, _____?
    A. didn't you   B. doesn't it
    C. aren't you   D. isn't it   【華江高中 1】

11. Edward's boss always _____ him do everything in the office.
    A. asks   B. chooses
    C. wants   D. makes   【復興高中 1】

12. Rainy days always make me _____.
    A. sad   B. to feel sad
    C. feeling sad   D. feeling sad   【中和高中 1】

13. Have some candy, _____ you?
    A. can   B. do
    C. won't   D. haven't   【西松高中 1】

14. Playing computer games never _____ me.
    A. bore   B. is good
    C. boring   D. bores   【西松高中 1】

15. That big house _____ Mr.Pitt.
    A. is belonged to
    B. was belonged to
    C. is belonging to
    D. belongs to   【台南女中 1】

16. He is _____ richer than I.
    A. ever   B. a lot of
    C. much   D. more   【和平高中】

17. I _____ Rachel to help me carry the heavy
shopping bags.
    A. got   B. let
    C. said   D. made   【北一女1】

18. My grandparents prefer to live in a house
_____ wood.
    A. making of
    B. making from
    C. made of
    D. made for   【華江高中1】

19. He is known _____ a great comedian.
    A. to   B. as
    C. for   D. by   【中正高中2】

20. You'd better get a mechanic _____ your
flat tire.
    A. fix   B. fixing
    C. fixed   D. to fix   【中正高中2】

21. _____ what to do, she cried.

    A. Not knowing

    B. Know

    C. Not known

    D. She didn't know　　　　　　　　【育成高中 1】

22. We heard the school bell _____ and ran.

    A. to ring　　　　　B. rang

    C. ringing　　　　　D. rung　　　　　【育成高中 1】

23. Mark _____ a lie.

    A. has seldom told

    B. always tell

    C. hardly never

    D. told often　　　　　　　　　【育成高中 1】

24. Customs vary from one culture to _____.

    A. the other　　　　B. others

    C. the others

    D. another　　　　　　　　　【和平高中 1】

25. This is a _____ job.

    A. tiring　　　　　B. tired

    C. tire　　　　　　D. to tire　　　【金陵女中 1】

26. The girl is _____ happy as a lark.

    A. so   B. very

    C. enough   D. as   【靜修女中 1】

27. Apples will turn brown when _____ to air.

    A. exposing   B. it is exposed

    C. exposed   D. exposure   【板橋高中 1】

28. Keep _____. You can make it.

    A. trying   B. to try

    C. to trying   D. and try   【靜修女中 1】

29. He was devoted _____ English for several years.

    A. himself to study

    B. to study

    C. to studying

    D. himself to studying   【基隆高中 1】

30. If World War III _____ tomorrow, what would we do?

    A. should happen

    B. is happened

    C. was happening

    D. has happened   【建中 1】

31. Not only you but she _____ to be moving.
    A. needs
    B. are
    C. have
    D. do
    【文德女中 1】

32. No one is _____ he may not learn.
    A. old that
    B. such old that
    C. so old as to
    D. so old that
    【南湖高中 1】

33. She wanted _____ the apartment decorated.
    A. having
    B. to have
    C. being
    D. to be
    【南湖高中 1】

34. I am sorry _____ you the other day.
    A. to offend
    B. having offended
    C. offending
    D. to have offended
    【南湖高中 1】

35. I don't know when he _____.
    A. will come
    B. to come
    C. has come
    D. coming
    【文華高中 1】

36. Mary _____ her report yet.

    A. finishes

    B. did finish

    C. hasn't finished

    D. has finished 【文華高中 1】

37. Study harder, _____ you can pass the test.

    A. or   B. otherwise

    C. if not   D. and 【台中二中 1】

38. _____ you like it or not, chocolate is always a treat.

    A. Whatever

    B. Whether

    C. Which

    D. What 【大安高工 1】

39. This is the house _____ I lived last year.

    A. when   B. in which

    C. that   D. which 【景美女中 2】

40. Many a boy and girl _____ come to school.

    A. were   B. was

    C. have   D. has 【清水高中 2】

41. Either orange _____ quite delicious.

    A. was   B. were

    C. has   D. have   【清水高中 2】

42. My family _____ at work now.

    A. being   B. are

    C. has   D. have   【清水高中 2】

43. Three months _____ a long time to wait for her to

    come.

    A. is   B. are

    C. has   D. have   【清水高中 2】

44. It is time that you _____ to bed.

    A. were   B. goes

    C. went   D. gone   【政大附中 1】

45. The little boy is growing _____.

    A. tall

    B. be tall

    C. to tall

    D. tallness   【南湖高中 1】

46. My friends _____ on the grass.
    A. lied   B. lain
    C. lay   D. laid   【復興高中 1】

47. He looked at me _____ I were a ghost.
    A. so that   B. if
    C. as if   D. in order that 【再興中學 1】

48. Vanessa's round face _____ a full moon.
    A. looks
    B. looks like
    C. tastes
    D. tastes like   【南山高中 1】

49. _____ that truth is stranger than fiction.
    A. People are said
    B. They are said
    C. It said
    D. It is said   【育成高中 1】

50. Jacky studies _____ harder than I do.
    A. greatly   B. very
    C. much   D. more   【新莊高中 1】

Test 10 詳解

1. **D** 只要他說實話，我會原諒他。

依句意，選 (D) *as long as*「只要」。

(A) → I *won't forgive* him *unless* he tells the truth.

除非他說實話，否則我不會原諒他。

2. **C** 自從我上次見到吉米已經二年了。

(D) → since I last saw。【詳見「文法寶典」p.492】

3. **C** 「物 + cost + 錢」表「某物值 (多少) 錢」。「人 + pay + for + 物」表「人付 (多少) 錢買物」。

【詳見「文法寶典」p.299】

4. **B** 「have been + V-ing」是現在完成進行式，加強「現在完成式」的語氣。【詳見「文法寶典」p.349】

5. **A** 他把他的成功歸因於他的父母和老師。

owe A to B 把 A 歸因於 B

6. **D** *even if*「即使」引導副詞子句，表讓步。

7. **A** since 的受詞須為特定時間，而不是一段時間。【詳見「文法寶典」p.493】

8. **A** 他的言行不一致。

agree with ①同意 (人)　②符合；一致

9. **C** 快一點，<u>否則</u>我們會錯過電影開始。【詳見「文法寶典」p.473】

10. **D** 名詞子句的附加問句，代名詞用 it。句尾的 isn't it?是
isn't it true?的省略。【詳見「文法寶典」p.6】

11. **D** 使役動詞 make 接受詞後，加原形動詞。(A) → asks him
to do。　　(C) → wants him ***to do***。

12. **A** make me (*be*) sad，使役動詞後面 be 省略。

13. **C** 肯定祈使句之後，***won't you*** 表「邀請」。【詳見「文法寶
典」p.6】

14. **D** 動名詞當主詞動詞用單數，bore 表「使厭倦」。

15. **D** ***belong to***　「屬於；歸屬」，沒有進行式和被動語態用法。

16. **C** very 修飾原級，much 修飾比較級。
【詳見「文法寶典」p.251】

17. **A** ***get sb. to + V.*** 使某人做某事
(B)、(D) 都是使役動詞，受詞後應用接原形動詞。

18. **C** My grandparents prefer to live in a house ***made of*** wood.
我祖父母比較喜歡住木造房子。
made of wood 源自 which is made of wood。
be made of 由～製成

19. **B**　他是著名的喜劇演員。

「*be known as* + 身分」表「以～身分而著名」、
「be known for + 特色」表「以～特色而著名」、
「be known to + 對象」表「為～對象所知」。

comedian〔kə'midɪən〕*n.* 喜劇演員

20. **D**　你最好找個機械工來修補你的爆胎。

mechanic〔mə'kænɪk〕*n.* 機械工　　*flat tire*　爆胎

21. **A**　<u>*Not knowing* what to do</u>, she cried.

不知道該怎麼辦，她哭了起來。

原句為：*Since she didn't know what to do*, she cried.，
副詞子句改分詞構句：① 去連接詞；② 去相同主詞；
③ V→V-ing，否定字 Not 要放在 V-ing 之前。
【詳見「文法寶典」p.458】

22. **C**　感官動詞 hear + 受詞 + 原形動詞/ Ving，表主動。
【詳見「文法寶典」p.278】

23. **A**　頻率副詞的位置：① be 動詞之後；② 一般動詞之前；
③ 助動詞和主要動詞之間。

(B) → always tells　　(C) *hardly ever*　很少（= *seldom*）
(D) → often told

24. **D**　*vary from one culture to another*　每個文化都不同
= *vary from culture to culture*

25. **A**　*tiring*　（事物）令人疲倦的，*tired*　（人）感到疲倦的。

26. **D** *(as) happy as a lark* 和雲雀一樣快樂；非常快樂

　　lark〔lɑrk〕*n.* 雲雀

27. **C** Apples will turn brown *when exposed to air.*

　　蘋果暴露在空氣中會變成棕色。

　　when *exposed* to

　　= when *they are exposed* to

　　when 引導的名詞子句中，句意明顯時，可省略主詞和

　　be 動詞。

28. **A** *keep + Ving* 持續做某事

29. **C** *be devoted to*

　　　= *devote oneself to* } + N/V-ing 致力於

30. **A** If 子句中用 *should*，表示可能性極小，作「萬一」解，爲

　　「與未來事實相反」的假設語氣。【詳見「文法寶典」p.363】

31. **A** not only...but also 連接兩個主詞時，動詞與靠近者一致。

　　【詳見「文法寶典」p.467】

32. **D** 沒有一個人是老到無法學習的。

　　so…that… 如此…以致於…【詳見「文法寶典」p.516】

33. **B** 她想要請人來裝潢公寓。

　　want 後接不定詞做受詞，have + O + p.p. 指「使~被…」，

　　表示「自己不做，叫別人做」。【詳見「文法寶典」p.387】

　　decorate〔'dɛkəˌret〕*v.* 裝飾；裝潢

34. **D** 很抱歉前幾天冒犯了你。

   the other day 前幾天，用不定詞完成式表示比主要動作早

   發生。【詳見「文法寶典」p.423】

35. **A** know 後面加上名詞子句，做受詞，表未來的事情，用未

   來式。

36. **C** yet 和否定的現在完成式連用，表「尚未」。

37. **D** 祈使句之後接 and 有「條件句」的作用。【詳見「文法寶典」

   p.466】

38. **B** 無論你喜不喜歡，巧克力總是能令人開心。

   whether...or（無論）引導表「讓步」的副詞子句。

   【詳見「文法寶典」p.524】　　　treat〔trit〕*n.* 樂事

39. **B** This is the house ***in which*** *I lived last year.*

   = This is the house ***where*** *I lived last year.*

   【詳見「文法寶典」p.243】

40. **D** Many a + 單 N + 單 V 許多

   = Many + 複 N + 複 V

41. **A** 這二顆柳橙任一顆都很美味。

   either 指「（二者中）任一」，後面接單數名詞再接單數動詞。

42. **B** 我的家人現在正在工作。

   family 在這裡表示一家人的家庭成員，本身為複數形。

   【詳見「文法寶典」p.50】　　***be at work*** 工作中

43. **A** 要等她來，三個月是一段很長的時間。

主詞 Three months 在此指「一段時間」，視爲單數，動詞亦用單數。

44. **C** It is time that you <u>went</u> to bed.

It is time that 後動詞用過去式，是「與現在事實相反」的假設語氣。【詳見「文法寶典」p.374】

45. **A** 「be growing + 形容詞」表「越來越…」。

46. **C**

lay-laid-laid-laying 下（蛋）；放置

lie-lay-lain-lying 躺；位在

lie-lied-lied-lying 說謊

> 記憶祕訣是：
> lay-laid-laid 變化和
> say-said-said 相同

依句意，選擇過去式的 (C) lay「躺」。

47. **C** 他看著我彷彿我是鬼一樣。

as if 表「好像」的假設法。【詳見「文法寶典」p.371】

48. **B** 依句意，選擇 (B) ***looks like***「看起來像…」，後面要加名詞。(A) looks「看起來」後面要加形容詞。

49. **D** 據說，事實比小說更離奇。

It is said that + 子句 = People say that + 子句，表「據說」之意。【詳見「文法寶典」p.371】

fiction〔ˈfɪkʃən〕*n.* 小說

50. **C** 程度副詞 ***much*** 用來強調比較級副詞。

【詳見「文法寶典」p.251】

TEST 11

1. The police _____ caught the thief.

   A. is　　　　　　B. are

   C. has　　　　　　D. have 【和平高中 1】

2. _____ you have is mine.

   A. Which　　　　　B. That

   C. Whatever

   D. No matter what 【大理高中 1】

3. _____ hard, and you'll keep the job and make

   money.

   A. Working　　　　B. Having worked

   C. Work　　　　　D. To work 【延平高中 1】

4. If only I _____ young again.

   A. am　　　　　　B. was

   C. were　　　　　D. should 【二信中學 1】

5. It _____ time to learn a new language.

   A. costs　　　　　B. makes

   C. spends　　　　D. takes 【三重高中 1】

6. The king is not kind _____ cruel.
   A. only　　　　　B. but
   C. also　　　　　D. not　　　　　【育成高中 1】

7. Mr. Rudolf insisted he _____ us home.
   A. drives　　　　B. drive
   C. driving
   D. to drive　　　　　【育成高中 1】

8. The man bought the vase which was _____ in Japan.
   A. makes　　　　B. making
   C. make　　　　　D. made　　　　【格致中學 1】

9. The joke _____ told by Bill many times.
   A. is　　　　　　B. x
   C. has been　　　D. has　　　　【南港高工 1】

10. I have spent _____ time on this project.
    A. a great deal of
    B. a great number of
    C. quite a few
    D. a wide range of　　　　【板橋高中 1】

11. What explains such mysterious _____?

    A. happenings

    B. happened

    C. happen

    D. happens   【內湖高中1】

12. It's better if you drink _____ water.

    A. boil   B. boiling

    C. boiled

    D. being boiled   【清水高中1】

13. The ball _____ was a soccer ball.

    A. used   B. using

    C. was used

    D. which used   【華江高中2】

14. The movie is worth _____.

    A. to be seen   B. seen

    C. to see   D. seeing   【成功高中2】

15. The 2012 Olympics were _____ in London.

    A. taken place   B. happened

    C. occurred

    D. held   【成功高中2】

16. No one knows _____.

    A. what to do   B. what do we say

    C. to go where   D. who to talk   【三民高中 1】

17. It isn't John's; it belongs to _____.

    A. a friend of mine

    B. a friend of me

    C. my friend's

    D. a friend's of mine   【弘文中學 1】

18. _____ air, we could not live.

    A. But for   B. With

    C. But   D. Except for   【文華高中】

19. Tom is _____ than brave.

    A. more wise   B. the wiser

    C. the more wise   D. wiser   【百齡高中 2】

20. His cancer _____ his long addiction to smoking.

    A. resulted in

    B. resulted from

    C. which caused by

    D. causing by   【南港高中 2】

21. My term paper is well on its way to _____.

    A. finish　　　　　B. being finished

    C. be finished　　　D. finishing　　　　　【景美女中 2】

22. Tom is _____ that we all like him.

    A. so honest boy

    B. a so honest boy

    C. so honest a boy

    D. so an honest boy　　　　　　　　　　【弘文中學 1】

23. The man _____ beside Julia is her husband.

    A. sitting at　　　　B. seats himself

    C. is seating　　　　D. seated　　　　　【百齡高中 1】

24. You _____ him a fool. He is really upset.

    A. shouldn't to call

    B. should call

    C. should have called

    D. shouldn't have called　　　　　　　　【弘文中學 1】

25. The more I learn, _____ I become.

    A. more interesting

    B. the interested

    C. the interesting

    D. the more interested　　　　　　　　【永春高中 1】

26. A friend _____ Michael called you last night.
    A. names   B. naming
    C. name   D. named   【中和高中 1】

27. We plan to paint our house _____.
    A. of pink   B. become blue
    C. at green   D. white   【中和高中 1】

28. If he _____ tomorrow, give me a call.
    A. is going to come B. comes
    C. came
    D. will come   【育成高中 1】

29. _____ being enthusiastic, John is always
    generous to others.
    A. Instead of
    B. In addition
    C. As a result
    D. Aside from   【基隆女中 1】

30. The patriot is the _____ person to betray
    our country.
    A. last   B. least
    C. late   D. latest   【成功高中 2】

31. Zack won't go with you, and _____.

    A. nor do I

    B. I won't, too

    C. I won't, neither

    D. neither will I   【三民高中 1】

32. English spelling always _____ me.

    A. confuses   B. confusing to

    C. confuse   D. confusing   【達人女中 1】

33. He _____ ill for a week when I visited him.

    A. had been   B. has

    C. had   D. is   【辭修高中 1】

34. My mother is busy _____ in the kitchen.

    A. cooking   B. to cook

    C. at cooking   D. cooked   【泰山高中 1】

35. You are not allowed _____ here.

    A. smoking

    B. to smoke

    C. smoke

    D. to be smoked   【中山女中 1】

36. The children _____ by the car were hurt.
  A. hit   B. who hit
  C. hitting   D. hits   【中崙高中1】

37. It is _____ of you to fool around after school.
  A. foolish   B. fool
  C. foolishness   D. fooling   【達人女中1】

38. _____ the future.
  A. There is no predicting
  B. No predicting
  C. When it comes to predicting
  D. Speaking of predicting   【成功高中1】

39. He has written three books _____.
  A. just now   B. in present
  C. a few years ago
  D. so far   【辭修高中1】

40. It's no use _____ over spilt milk.
  A. to cry
  B. of crying
  C. crying
  D. to be crying   【中崙高中1】

41. When I saw the fire, I _____ the fire department.

    A. call   B. will call

    C. called   D. calling   【華僑高中 1】

42. The following _____ stories about a ship.

    A. is   B. are

    C. have   D. has   【華僑高中 1】

43. A teacher is often _____ a person who assigns homework.

    A. think as

    B. thought of as

    C. thinking of

    D. thought as   【南港高中 1】

44. My parents won't let me _____ the party.

    A. have gone   B. to go

    C. going   D. go to   【基隆高中 1】

45. I like _____ you cook for me.

    A. whomever

    B. whichever

    C. whatever

    D. wherever   【清水高中 1】

46. I don't like this kind of shirt. Could you show me
    _____?
    A. one   B. another one
    C. the other   D. other one   【基隆高中 1】

47. Comets _____ to be a sign of disaster.
    A. were thought
    B. were thinking
    C. were to think
    D. thought   【中崙高中 1】

48. Another difficulty arose _____ we were trying to
    solve this problem.
    A. while   B. no sooner
    C. therefore   D. if   【南港高中 1】

49. Did he mention to you that he'd go _____ after
    graduation?
    A. bread   B. abroad
    C. board   D. aboard   【內湖高中 1】

50. To keep good hours _____ one healthy.
    A. is making   B. is made
    C. makes   D. make   【清水高中 1】

Test 11 詳解

1. **D** 本題時態應為現在完成式，*the police*「警方」為複數，
故助動詞應用 *have*，選 (D)。

2. **C** ***Whatever you have*** is mine.
　　　名 詞 子 句
你所有的一切都是我的。

複合關代 Whatever 引導名詞子句，做 is 的主詞，
Whatever 等於 Anything that。No matter what 引導副
詞子句，文法不合。

3. **C** Work hard, ***and*** you'll keep the job and make money.
努力工作，你就可以保有工作並賺到錢。

「祈使句，*and*⋯」表「肯定條件」。【詳見「文法寶典」p.360】

4. **C** 要是我能再次年輕就好了！

If only「要是～就好了」，表示不可能實現的願望，所以
用假設語氣，與現在事實相反，be 動詞用 *were*，選 (C)。
【詳見「文法寶典」p.370】

5. **D** It takes time *to learn a new language*.
學習一個新的語言需要時間。

It 為虛主詞，真正主詞為不定詞片語，事物「花費」時
間，動詞用 *takes*，選 (D)。【詳見「文法寶典」p.299】

6. **B** 國王不仁慈，<u>而是</u>很殘忍。

　　not A but B 不是 A 而是 B　　cruel〔'kruəl〕*adj.* 殘忍的

7. **B** insist「堅持」是慾望動詞，後接名詞子句中，動詞用 should + V原，而 should 常省略。【詳見「文法寶典」p.313】

8. **D** The man bought the vase *which was <u>made</u> in Japan.*
　　那位男士買了這個在日本製作的花瓶。

　　依句意爲被動，應用 be + p.p.，選 (D) *made*。

9. **C** 表示從過去一直到現在的經驗，用「現在完成式」，依句意爲被動，選 (C) *has been*。【詳見「文法寶典」p.335】

10. **A** 我已經在這個計劃上花費了<u>很多</u>時間。

$$\left\{\begin{array}{l}\textit{a great deal of }\text{ 很多；大量【接不可數名詞】}\\ \text{a great number of } \text{很多}\\ \text{quite a few } \text{很多}\\ \text{a wide range of } \text{各種}\end{array}\right\} \text{【接可數複數名詞】}$$

11. **A** 如此神祕的<u>事情</u>要怎麼解釋？

　　such 當形容詞，指「如此的；這樣的」，後面要接名詞。
　　happening〔'hæpənɪŋ〕*n.* 事情

12. **C** 如果你喝<u>已經煮沸的</u>水是比較好的。

　　依句意，選 (C) *boiled*「已經煮沸的」，(B) boiling「正在沸騰的」，不合句意。

13. **A**　The ball *used* was a soccer ball.

所使用的球是一顆足球。

依句意選 (A) *used*，源自於形容詞子句 *which was used*。

14. **D**　The movie is worth seeing.

這部電影值得一看。

be worth + *V-ing*「值得…」，動名詞有三個條件：①主動②及物動詞③無受詞。

15. **D**　The 2012 Olympics were held *in London*.

2012 奧運會在倫敦舉行。

> *take place*　發生；舉行【均為不及物用法，沒有被動】
> = happen
> = occur

hold「舉行」，為及物動詞，被動為 *be held*。

16. **A**　No one knows *what to do*.

沒有人知道該怎麼辦。

疑問詞 + 不定詞，形成名詞片詞，做 knows 的受詞。

(B) → what to say

(C) → where to go

(D) → who(m) to talk to【詳見「文法寶典」p.418】

17. **A** 那不是約翰的；那屬於<u>我的一位朋友</u>。

a 和所有格名詞修飾同一個名詞，要用「雙重所有格」：
a friend of mine 我的一位朋友。【詳見「文法寶典」p.97】
(C) → my friend ***belong to*** 屬於

18. **A** <u>如果沒有</u>空氣，我們就無法生存。

but for 如果沒有（ = *without* ）
(D) except for 除了～之外，句意不合。

19. **A** Tom is ***more*** wise ***than*** brave.
與其說湯姆勇敢，不如說他有智慧。

同一人二種性質做比較時，一律用 ***more～than***… 表示，
做「與其說…，不如說～」解。【詳見「文法寶典」p.201】

20. **B** His cancer <u>resulted from</u> his long addiction *to smoking*.
他的癌症<u>起因於</u>他長期的煙癮。

result from 起因於（ = *be caused by* ）
(A) result in 導致；造成（ = *cause* ）
addiction〔ə'dɪkʃən〕*n.* 上癮 < *to* >

21. **B** 我的期末報告快要完成了。

on its way to 字面意思是「去～途中」，在此引申為「接
近」，to 是介系詞，後接名詞或動名詞，而依句意，報告
「完成」要用 be finished，故本題選 (B) ***being finished***。
term paper 期末報告

22. **C** Tom is *so honest a boy that we all like him.*

湯姆是如此誠實的男孩，我們都喜歡他。

= Tom is *such an honest boy* that we all like him.

= Tom is *so honest* that we all like him.

【詳見「文法寶典」p.517】

23. **D** The man _seated beside Julia_ is her husband.

坐在茱莉亞旁邊的那位男士是她的丈夫。

分詞片語 *seated* beside Julia 來自形容詞子句 *who is seated* beside Julia。形容詞子句也可用 *who is sitting* beside Julia，省略而成 *sitting* beside Julia。

24. **D** 你當時不應該叫他笨蛋的，他現在很難過。

shouldn't have + p.p. 表示「過去不該做但已做」。

【詳見「文法寶典」p.364】

25. **D** 我學得越多，就變得越有興趣。

The + 比較級~，the + 比較級… 越~，就越…

形容人「有興趣的」應用 interested，故選 (D) *the more interested*。

26. **D** A friend _named Michael_ called you *last night.*

一位名叫麥克的朋友昨晚打電話給你。

A friend *named* Michael 源自於 A friend *who was named* Michael。

27. **D** We plan to paint <u>our house</u> <u>white</u>.
　　　　　　　　　　　　受　詞　　　　受補

我們計劃把房子漆成白色。

28. **B** *If he <u>comes</u> tomorrow*, give me a call.

如果他明天來了，打個電話給我。

表「條件」的副詞子句中，要用現在式代替未來式，選
(B) *comes*。

29. **D** <u>Aside from</u> being enthusiastic, John is *always* generous

to others.

除了熱心<u>之外</u>，約翰對他人也總是很慷慨。

$$\begin{cases} \textbf{\textit{aside from}} \ \ 除了～之外 \\ = \textbf{\textit{in addition to}} \\ = \textbf{\textit{besides}} \end{cases}$$

(A) instead of　而非

(C) as a result　因此

30. **A** 這位愛國志士是最不可能背叛我們國家的人。

be the last to V.　是最不可能～的

patriot〔ˋpetrɪət〕 *n.* 愛國者　　betray〔bɪˋtre〕 *v.* 背叛

31. **D** Zack won't go with you, and *neither will I*.

柴克不會和你去，我也不會。

= Zack won't go with you, and *I won't either*.

= Zack won't go with you, *nor will I*.

【詳見「文法寶典」p.133】

32. **A** English spelling always *confuses* me.

英文拼字總是<u>使</u>我<u>困惑</u>。

= I am always *confused* about English spelling.

= English spelling is always *confusing* to me.

confuse「使困惑」是情感動詞，人做主詞，形容詞用 confused「感到困惑的」，形容事物「令人困惑的」，用 confusing。

33. **A** He <u>had been</u> ill *for a week when I visited him*.

當我去看他時，他已經病了一星期了。

表某事從過去稍早，到過去某時已有一段時間，用「過去完成式」。【詳見「文法寶典」p.338】

34. **A** *be busy* (*in*) *V-ing* 忙於

35. **B** *be allowed to* + *V* 被允許做某事

36. **A** The children *hit by the car* were hurt.

被車撞到的孩子們受傷了。

hit by the car 源自 *who were hit* by the car。

37. **A** It is <u>foolish</u> of you to fool around *after school.*

你放學後游手好閒是很<u>愚蠢的</u>。

空格應填形容詞，選 (A) *foolish*「愚蠢的」。
fool around 游手好閒；閒混

38. **A** <u>There is no predicting</u> the future. 未來無法預測。

= It is impossible to predict the future.
There is no + V-ing ～是不可能的
predict〔prɪ'dɪkt〕*v.* 預測

39. **D** 依句意選 (D) *so far*「到目前為止」，和現在完成式連用。

(A) just now 剛才；現在
(B) → in the present 或 at present 現在
(C) a few years ago 幾年前【和過去式連用】

40. **C** It's no use <u>crying</u> over spilt milk.

為了打翻的牛奶而哭是沒有用的；【諺】覆水難收。

It is no use + V-ing 做～是沒有用的
spilt〔spɪlt〕*adj.* 打翻的；溢出的

41. **C** *When I saw the fire*, I <u>called</u> the fire department.

當我看到火災，我打電話給消防隊。

依句意為過去式，選 (C) *called*。

42. **B** *The following* $\left\{\begin{array}{l} \text{is} + \text{單數 N} \\ \text{are} + \text{複數 N} \end{array}\right.$ 以下是~

43. **B** A teacher is *often* <u>thought of as</u> a person *who assigns*

homework. 老師常被認為是指派作業的人。

$\left\{\begin{array}{l} \textbf{think of } A \textbf{ as } B \ \text{認為 A 是 B} \\ = \text{think A (to be) B} \end{array}\right.$

改被動則成為：$\left\{\begin{array}{l} \textbf{A be thought of as } B \ \text{A 被認為是 B} \\ = \text{A be thought to be B} \end{array}\right.$

assign〔ə'saɪn〕*v.* 指派

44. **D** 使役動詞 let 接受詞後接原形動詞。

45. **C** I like *whatever you cook for me*.
名　詞　子　句

只要是你為我煮的菜我都喜歡。

複合關代 *whatever* 引導名詞子句，做 like 的受詞，在子句中又做 cook 的受詞，whatever 相當於 anything that。

46. **B** { another one
          = a different one 【詳見「文法寶典」p.140】

   (C) the other 是「（二者中）的另一」，在此句意不合。

47. **A** Comets <u>were thought</u> to be a sign *of disaster.*

   彗星<u>被認</u>爲是災難的徵兆。

   請參照第 43 題。

   comet〔'kɑmɪt〕*n.* 彗星　　sign〔saɪn〕*n.* 徵兆
   disaster〔dɪz'æstɚ〕*n.* 災難

48. **A** Another difficulty arose ***while*** *we were trying to solve*

   this problem.

   當我們試著解決這個問題時，另一個困難出現了。

   依句意選 (A) ***while***，表「當～時」。
   arise〔ə'raɪz〕*v.* 發生；出現【三態變化爲：arise-arose-arisen】

49. **B** 他有沒有向你提到，他畢業後就要出國呢？

   go abroad 出國

50. **C** <u>To keep good hours</u> <u>makes</u> one healthy.
         　　　　S　　　　　　　V.

   早睡早起使人健康。

   不定詞做主詞，爲單數，動詞亦用單數，故選 (C) ***makes***。
   keep good hours 早睡早起

TEST 12

1. Is there ＿＿＿＿＿ at school?

   A. anything special

   B. special anything

   C. good things

   D. things good　　　　　　　　　　　【萬芳高中 1】

2. Playing computer games ＿＿＿＿＿ a lot of fun.

   A. is　　　　　　　B. has

   C. are　　　　　　　D. have　　　　　　【萬芳高中 1】

3. He woke up early ＿＿＿＿＿ catch the first bus.

   A. so that　　　　　B. in order that

   C. with a view to　　D. in order to　　　【基隆高中 1】

4. Larry hasn't been to Japan, ＿＿＿＿＿.

   A. nor has Mary　　B. nor was Mary

   C. Mary has, too

   D. nor does Mary　　　　　　　　　　【萬芳高中 1】

5. I saw the naughty boy ＿＿＿＿＿ by his dad.

   A. punishment　　B. being punished

   C. to be punish　　D. punish　　　　【清水高中 1】

6. You have to go there, but I _____.
   A. won't   B. haven't
   C. am not
   D. don't
   【萬芳高中 1】

7. He is punished for _____ he does.
   A. which   B. that
   C. so
   D. what
   【清水高中 1】

8. I cannot speak English _____ Candie.
   A. as well as
   B. to well as
   C. too good as
   D. as good as
   【永春高中 1】

9. David denied _____ the money.
   A. had stolen   B. stealing
   C. to steal
   D. stole
   【永春高中 1】

10. The garbage should _____ out. It smells.
    A. be taken   B. be taking
    C. took   D. take
    【永春高中 1】

11. Joseph is always ＿＿＿＿ competition with Amy for
　　 first prize in our class.
　　 A. up　　　　　　B. on
　　 C. in　　　　　　D. at　　　　　【內湖高中 1】

12. I never ＿＿＿＿ if I fail to win the prize.
　　 A. fall badly
　　 B. feel bad
　　 C. feel badly
　　 D. fell bad　　　　　　　　　【和平高中 1】

13. Having many good friends ＿＿＿＿ happiness to me.
　　 A. means　　　　　B. meaning
　　 C. meant　　　　　D. mean　　　【麗山高中 1】

14. Why not ＿＿＿＿ him Albert?
　　 A. naming　　　　　B. to name
　　 C. be named　　　　D. name　　　【麗山高中 1】

15. You should avoid ＿＿＿＿ mistakes again.
　　 A. to make　　　　B. making
　　 C. make　　　　　D. made　　　【三重高中 1】

16. The naughty boy played a trick _____ me.
   A. in   B. to
   C. on   D. for   【三重高中 1】

17. How long has it been since you _____ a raise in salary?
   A. have had   B. had
   C. have   D. has   【南湖高中 1】

18. On the next anniversary, they _____ married for 30 years.
   A. have been   B. be
   C. would have
   D. will have been   【南湖高中 1】

19. If I _____ you, I would not stay in this company anymore.
   A. was   B. were
   C. am   D. are   【南湖高中 1】

20. I wrote to Tom, _____ him for his help.
   A. thank   B. thanking
   C. and thanks   D. thanked   【華江高中 1】

21. John is a friend of _____.

    A. my　　　　　　　B. his

    C. their's　　　　　D. her　　　　　　【萬芳高中 1】

22. I wish I _____ in Japan last year.

    A. was　　　　　　B. had been

    C. were　　　　　　D. am　　　　　　【萬芳高中 1】

23. The only thing he likes to do _____ the violin.

    A. was play　　　　B. is play

    C. playing　　　　　D. to play　　　　【大安高工 1】

24. _____ he told you isn't true.

    A. That　　　　　　B. What

    C. Whether　　　　　D. How　　　　　【西松高中 1】

25. Ann is the only student _____ passed the test.

    A. that　　　　　　B. which

    C. whom　　　　　　D. whose　　　　【西松高中 1】

26. What's _____ the lake?

    A. to pollute　　　　B. polluted

    C. polluting　　　　D. pollute　　　【三重高中 1】

27. There _____ no more bargains, she left disappointed.

    A. was   B. had been

    C. is   D. being   【再興中學 1】

28. The house built 100 years ago seems _____ now.

    A. deserting   B. deserts

    C. deserted   D. desert   【再興中學 1】

29. Her baby is ill at home, _____ she goes to work.

    A. although   B. and

    C. but   D. so   【西松高中 1】

30. This is the reason _____ I don't like you.

    A. why   B. where

    C. how   D. which   【清水高中 1】

31. The book is of great value. _____ can be enjoyed unless you digest it.

    A. Nothing

    B. Something

    C. Everything

    D. Anything   【中國福建高考】

32. Dressing babies _____ wrapping up expensive china.

    A. is like

    B. is likes

    C. likes

    D. were like　　　　　　　　　　　　【聖心女中 1】

33. Bamboo _____ many kinds of products, ranging from T-shirts to beds.

    A. used to making

    B. is used to making

    C. used to make

    D. is used to make　　　　　　　　　　【板橋高中 1】

34. Are you going to leave the door _____?

    A. opened　　　　　　B. close

    C. open　　　　　　　D. opening　　　【三重高中 1】

35. The dishes your mother cooked _____.

    A. were tasted great

    B. are tasted deliciously

    C. tasted delicious

    D. tasted greatly　　　　　　　　　　【泰北高中 1】

36. He looked _____ at me and said nothing to me.
    A. angry   B. angrily
    C. anger   D. happy   【三重高中 1】

37. When we arrived at the airport, the plane _____.
    A. leaves
    B. was being left
    C. has left
    D. had left   【西松高中 1】

38. There will be a time _____ we get together again.
    A. who   B. which
    C. whenever   D. when   【清水高中 1】

39. The vacation _____ over, the students came back
    to school.
    A. is   B. are
    C. being   D. was   【再興中學 1】

40. Many students, _____ Laura, liked the new
    principal.
    A. included   B. include
    C. inclusive   D. including   【再興中學 1】

41. It was _____ who talked to Jason.

   A. I   B. me

   C. my   D. mine   【徐匯中學 1】

42. No one knows the solution _____ the problem.

   A. of   B. to

   C. by   D. with   【新店高中 1】

43. Reactions _____ more slowly at lower temperatures.

   A. are happened   B. took place

   C. hold   D. occur   【聖心女中 1】

44. The program _____ many people.

   A. is satisfied

   B. satisfies

   C. satisfying

   D. satisfy   【萬芳高中 1】

45. The news of his success _____ his parents.

   A. delighting

   B. to be delighted

   C. delighted

   D. delight   【三重高中 1】

46. What _____ you buy if you won the lottery?

    A. would   B. will

    C. did   D. do   【聖心女中 1】

47. He can catch the ball with one hand and hit with

    _____.

    A. another   B. other

    C. the other   D. others   【靜修女中 1】

48. What _____ you cry?

    A. caused   B. cause

    C. made   D. get   【永平高中 1】

49. The air expands when _____.

    A. heat   B. heated

    C. heats   D. hitting   【靜修女中 1】

50. Everyone _____ his funny big hat.

    A. couldn't help but notice

    B. couldn't help notice

    C. couldn't but noticing

    D. had not choice but notice   【永平高中 1】

Test 12　詳解

1. **A**　something, anything, nothing 等字，形容詞要放在後面。

2. **A**　<u>Playing computer games</u> <u>is</u> a lot of fun.
　　　　　　　　　S　　　　　　　　V.

　　玩電腦遊戲非常有趣。

　　be fun「有趣」，動名詞做主詞，為單數，故用單數動詞 ***is***，選 (A)。

3. **D**　He woke up *early in order to catch the first bus.*

　　他早起，為了趕第一班公車。

　　表「目的」的用法：$\begin{cases} \text{so that} + 子句 \\ \text{in order that} + 子句 \\ \text{with a view to} + \text{V-ing} \\ \textbf{\textit{in order to}} + \textbf{\textit{V}} \end{cases}$
　　【詳見「文法寶典」p.514】

4. **A**　Larry hasn't been to Japun, <u>nor *has* Mary</u>.
　　= Larry hasn't been to Japan, <u>and Mary *hasn't*,</u> either.
　　賴瑞沒去過日本，瑪麗也沒有。

　　前後兩句時態要一致，助動詞用 ***has***。

5. **B**　我看見那個頑皮的男孩被他爸爸處罰。

　　依句意「被處罰」為被動，選 (B) ***being punished***。
　　naughty〔ˋnɔtɪ〕*adj.* 頑皮的

6. **D** 你必須去那裡，但是我不必。

空格原應為 I don't have to go there，簡略為 ***I don't***。
have to + V「必須」的否定為：don't have to + V
「不必」。

7. **D** He is punished for ***what*** he does.
他因他所做的事而受罰。

複合關代 ***what*** 引導名詞子句，做 for 的受詞。

8. **A** I cannot speak English *as well as Candie.*

我說英文沒有坎蒂好。

9. **B** deny〔dɪˈnaɪ〕*v.* 否認，***deny + V-ing*** 表「否認做過某事」
之意。

10. **A** 垃圾應該拿出去倒了。它都發臭了。

依句意要用被動，選 (A) ***be taken***。
smell〔smɛl〕*v.* 有臭味

11. **C** Joseph is *always* in competition *with Amy for first prize*

in our class.

約瑟夫和艾咪在我們班上，總是在爭奪第一名。
be in competition with sb. for sth. 和某人競爭，爭奪某物

12. **B** I *never* <u>feel bad</u> *if I fail to win the prize.*

即使沒有得獎，我也絕不會覺得難過。

feel「覺得」在此為不完全不及物動詞，接形容詞做主詞
補語，選 (B) *feel bad*「覺得難過」。
(A) fall–fell–fallen 落下
(D) fell–felled–felled 砍伐，句意、用法均不合。

13. **A** <u>Having many good friends</u> <u>means</u> happiness to me.
　　　　　　　S　　　　　　　　　V.

有許多好朋友，對我來說，意謂著快樂。

動名詞當主詞，為單數，依句意為現在式，動詞用 *means*，
選 (A)。

14. **D** Why not <u>name</u> him Albert?

何不將他取名為亞伯特？

Why not +V原 源自於 *Why* do*n't* you/we +V原，表「建議」。

15. **B** 你應該避免再次犯錯。

avoid「避免」，後接動名詞做受詞。

16. **C** *play a trick on sb.* 對某人惡作劇

17. **B** How long has it been *since you <u>had</u> a raise in salary*?

自從你加薪以來已經多久了？

since「自從」引導的副詞子句，要用過去式，主要子句要用現在完成式。

raise〔rez〕*n.* 增加；加薪　　salary〔'sælərɪ〕*n.* 薪水

18. **D** *On the next anniversary*, they will have been married *for 30 years.*

在明年的結婚紀念日，他們將結婚 30 年了。

表示到未來某時，動作將已經完成，用「未來完成式」。

【詳見「文法寶典」p.340】

anniversary〔͵ænə'vɝsərɪ〕*n.* 週年紀念；在此指「結婚紀念日」

19. **B** *If I were you*, I would not stay *in this company anymore.*

如果我是你，我不會再留在這家公司了。

依句意「如果我是你」，但我不可能是你，If 子句中，與現在事實相反，be 動詞要用 *were*，選 (B)。【詳見「文法寶典」p.361】

20. **B** I wrote to Tom, thanking him *for his help.*

我寫信給湯姆，感謝他幫忙。

本句原為 I wrote to Tom *and thanked* him for his help. 省略 and，把 thanked 改成 *thanking*，形成分詞構句。

【詳見「文法寶典」p.457】

21. **B** 「雙重所有格」的用法為：

a + N + *of* + 所有格名詞【詳見「文法寶典」p.97】

a friend of his 他的一位朋友

(A) → mine　(C) → theirs　(D) hers

22. **B** wish 表示「不可能實現的願望」，要用假設法，由時間 last year 可知，為「與過去事實相反」，要用 *had been*，選 (B)。【詳見「文法寶典」p.368】

23. **B** The only thing *he likes to do* is play the violin.

他唯一喜歡做的事就是拉小提琴。

The only thing (the first thing, all 等) + one has to do is 之後的不定詞 to 可有可無，美式英語多把 to 省略。【詳見「文法寶典」p. 419, 648】

24. **B** ___*What he told you*___ isn't true. 他告訴你的事情不是真的。
　　　　名 詞 子 句

複合關代 What 引導名詞子句，做主詞，What 等於 The thing that。

25. **A** Ann is the only student ___*that*___ *passed the test.*

安是唯一通過測驗的學生。

先行詞中有 the only 時，關代通常用 *that*。【詳見「文法寶典」p.153】

26. **C** 是什麼在污染這座湖？

空格中爲句子的主要動詞，What's 爲 What is 的縮寫，is 後應用現在分詞，形成現在進行式，故選 (C) *polluting*。

27. **D** *There being no more bargains*, she left *disappointed*.

主 補

特價品沒有了，她失望地離開。

副詞子句原爲 *Since there were* no more bargains，省略連接詞，改成分詞構句，變成 *There being* no more bargains，disappointed 用形容詞，爲主詞補語，補充說明主詞。 bargain〔'bɑrgɪn〕 *n.* 廉價品；特價品

28. **C** The house *built 100 years ago* seems deserted *now*.

這棟 100 年前蓋的房子，現在似乎荒廢了。

seem「似乎」後接形容詞做補語，依句意選 (C) *deserted*「被遺棄的；荒廢的」。

29. **C** 她的寶寶生病在家，但是她還是去工作。

依句意選 (C) *but*。

30. **A** This is the reason *why I don't like you.*

這就是爲什麼我不喜歡你的原因。

關係副詞 why 引導形容詞子句，修飾先行詞 the reason。

31. **A** The book is of great value. <u>Nothing</u> can be enjoyed
unless you digest it.

這本書非常有價值。除非你把書消化完了,否則享受不到任何
東西。

依句意選 (A) *Nothing*。　　　digest〔 daɪˈdʒɛst 〕 *v.* 消化

> *of great value* 非常有價值
> = very valuable

32. **A** Dressing babies <u>is like</u> wrapping up expensive china.

幫小寶寶穿衣服,就像在包裝昂貴的瓷器。

依句意選 (A) *is like*,like 做「像」解,是介系詞,前面
和動詞連用。　　　dress〔 drɛs 〕 *v.* 使穿衣

wrap up 包裝　　　china〔ˈtʃaɪnə 〕 *n.* 瓷器

33. **D** Bamboo <u>is used to make</u> many kinds of products, *ranging from T-shirts to beds.*

竹子<u>被用來製作</u>許多種產品,從 T 恤到床都有。

> *be used to V* 被用來~
> *used to V* 過去常常~;過去曾經~
> *be used to V-ing* 習慣於

34. **C** 你要任由門開著嗎?

leave 是不完全及物動詞,接受詞後接受詞補語,表示門
「開著」或「關著」,用 *open* 或 closed,選 (C)。

35. **C** The dishes *your mother cooked* <u>tasted delicious</u>.

你媽媽煮的菜很好吃。

taste「吃起來」後面要接形容詞。

36. **B** 他<u>生氣地</u>看著我，沒有對我說任何話。

修飾動詞用副詞，選 (B) *angrily*。

37. **D** ***When*** *we arrived at the airport*, the plane <u>had left</u>.

當我們到達機場時，飛機已經離開了。

過去的過去用「過去完成式」。【詳見「文法寶典」p.338】

38. **D** There will be a time ***when*** *we get together again.*

我們會再相聚的。

關係副詞 when 引導形容詞子句，修飾先行詞 time。

39. **C** *The vacation <u>being</u> over*, the students came back to school. 假期結束了，學生們都回到了學校。

此句原為：***Since/After*** *the vacation **was** over*, the students.... 副詞子句改分詞構句：①去連接詞②主詞 the vacation 和主要子句不同，保留③ was→***being***。

40. **D** 許多學生，包括蘿拉，都喜歡這位新校長。

$$\left\{\begin{array}{l} \textbf{\textit{including}} \text{ Laura} \quad 包括蘿拉 \\ = \textbf{\textit{inclusive of}} \text{ Laura} \\ = \text{Laura } \textbf{\textit{included}} \end{array}\right.$$

principal〔ˈprɪnsəpl̩〕 *n.* 校長

41. **A** It was I who talked to Jason. 就是我和傑森談話的。

本句原為：I talked to Jason.
利用強調句型：*It is/was* + 強調部分 + *that* + 其餘部分，
強調主詞 I，而將 I 放在 was 之後，強調部分為人，故
that 可用 *who* 代替。【詳見「文法寶典」p.115】

42. **B** *the solution to the problem* 問題的解決方法

43. **D** Reactions occur *more slowly at lower temperatures*.

溫度較低時，反應發生較慢。

happen, *take place*, *occur* 均為「發生」之意，是不及物用
法，要用主動，而本句為真理，應用現在簡單式，故選 (D)。

44. **B** 這個計劃使很多人滿意。

本句需要動詞，且依句意為主動，用情感動詞 satisfy
「使滿意」，這句話也可寫成：
The program is *satisfying* to many people.
（這個計劃令許多人滿意。）
Many people are *satisfied* with the program.
（許多人對這個計劃感到滿意。）

45. **C** 他成功的消息<u>使</u>他父母很<u>高興</u>。

同上題，這句話也可寫成：

His parents were *delighted* at the news of his success.

但注意，delighting 沒有形容詞的用法。

46. **A** 如果你中了樂透，你要買什麼？

與現在事實相反的假設語氣，if 子句用過去式，主要子句則用 *would*/could/should/might + 原形 V，選 (A)。

47. **C** He can catch the ball *with one hand* **and** hit *with <u>the other</u>*.

他可以用一手接球，另一手擊球。

表示「（二者中）另一個」用 *the other*，選 (C)。

48. **C** 什麼事情惹你哭了？

根據受詞後 cry 用原形可知，空格應用使役動詞，選 (C) *made*。

49. **B** The air expands *when <u>heated</u>*. 空氣受熱會膨脹。

when heated 源自 *when it is heated*。

heat〔hit〕*v.* 加熱；使變熱

50. **A** 每個人不禁都注意到他那頂好笑的大帽子。

$$\left\{ \begin{array}{l} \textbf{\textit{cannot help but}} + \textbf{\textit{V}} \quad \text{忍不住；不禁} \\ = \textbf{\textit{cannot help}} + \textbf{\textit{V-ing}} \\ = \textbf{\textit{cannot but}} + \textbf{\textit{V}} \\ = \textbf{\textit{have no choice but to}} + \textbf{\textit{V}} \end{array} \right.$$

編後感言

上了六週文法試題後，感謝蔡琇瑩老師和謝靜芳老師，每次上課辛苦寫黑板。語言千變萬化，有人說A，有人說B，我們採取大部分主流，如：

Carl was seen ＿＿＿＿ the building last night. 【p.12】
A. enter　　　　　　　B. entering
C. to enter　　　　　　D. having entered

這條題目，大陸老師常問，答案應該是(C)才對啊！感官動詞改成被動，後面原形要改成不定詞 to enter。

【主動】 Someone saw Carl enter the building last night. 〔正〕
【被動】 Carl was seen to enter the building last night. 〔誤〕

事實上，無意中看到或聽到的要用現在分詞，不可用不定詞，如：

I like to hear her *sing*. 〔正，特意〕
Yesterday I passed by her room. I heard her *singing*. 〔正，無意〕

在這條題目中，Carl was seen 是無意中被看到，所以用現在分詞，不可用不定詞，在「文法寶典」中有明確的說明。

不管文法學得多精、多徹底，往往有例外，好在我們發明了「一口氣考試英語」，把文法試題變成會話，刁鑽的句子

編成會話，英語說起來很有深度。例如有一次，我在德國，投宿一家旅館，房卡故障，無法進門，我找了櫃台更換，依然無效，跑上跑下跑了三次，櫃台請人來修理，我等了很久，於是我說：

> I've been here an hour. 我已經在這裡一小時。
> It seems like foerever. 似乎好像很久了。
> I don't feel like waiting any longer. 【日本早大】
> 我不想再等了。

一般同學都知道 feel like + V-ing，但不會用在會話中，「啞巴英語」是世紀的癌症，是所有學英文的人共同的痛苦，這種新方法，讓同學會說話又會考試。

我教授升大學英語 40 多年，發現現在的高中生，受到「啞巴英語」的摧殘，不想開口說，上課已經僵硬到懶得站起來，叫他們用英文呼口號，更是讓他們痛苦萬分，每一個人被考試壓得喘不過氣來。我們發明的「一口氣考試英語」，讓同學站起來一起呼喊，甚至走出教室上課。平常我們說慣中文，大聲說出英文，才能改變嘴部發音肌肉，這是一項突破，一旦死氣沈沈的學生復活，所產生的能量驚人。

我們現在正在教授「一口氣考試英語」，感觸良多，每次上課 81 句，以三句為一組、九句為一回，共九回，有劇情，經過實驗，林工富老師二小時就能唸完 81 句，其餘英文老師也接近九成。如果同學一週背 81 句，六週下來就背了 486 句，有了這些句子，就有信心開口說英文，也可以輕鬆應考了。

做試題和背會話，交叉練習，學的是活的英語，句子分析法是解題的捷徑，所以每條題目我們都儘可能分析，讓同學能夠找出句子的主詞和動詞，學會句子分析法有助於閱讀和寫作。本書還可搭配「六週文法試題班」講座實況 DVD，希望有老師跟著學，把這個方法傳出去。

我曾經帶過蔡琇瑩老師和謝靜芳老師，去大陸舉行英文師資培訓，對於大陸的英文老師求知若渴的精神，很感動，值得我們學習。很感謝「中國教育培訓聯盟」牛新哲主席的邀請，才有機會把每年的新發明，分享給其他英文老師。好的老師，上課每分鐘都很重要，讓同學在最短時間內學最多東西，要有無數的訣竅，每三分鐘就有一次高潮，要不斷讓同學興奮與滿足。我很慶幸，能夠不斷地研究發明，上課實驗後再編輯成書。

英雄所見略同，日本和大陸升大學考題，和台灣試題比較，常有雷同之處。做完日本、大陸試題，再做台灣的試題就簡單了。雖然這些全真試題，是出題老師嘔心瀝血的結晶，有時難免還是會出現中式英語，這些我們都加以改正。感謝在美國任教的 Laura Stewart 老師，每天和我一起工作的 Christian Adams 老師，以及 Edward McGuire 老師，他們認真長期工作，更要感謝一起工作 25 年的蔡琇瑩老師和謝靜芳老師，為了語言革命，我們會拼到最後一分鐘。全書雖經審慎校對，仍恐有疏漏之處，敬請各界先進不吝指正。

編者 謹識

全真文法 450 題詳解

主　　　編 / 劉　毅

發　行　所 / 學習出版有限公司　　☎ (02) 2704-5525

郵 撥 帳 號 / 05127272 學習出版社帳戶

登　記　證 / 局版台業 2179 號

印　刷　所 / 裕強彩色印刷有限公司

台 北 門 市 / 台北市許昌街 10 號 2F　　☎ (02) 2331-4060

台灣總經銷 / 紅螞蟻圖書有限公司　　☎ (02) 2795-3656

本 公 司 網 址　www.learnbook.com.tw

電 子 郵 件　learnbook@learnbook.com.tw

> 售價：新台幣二百八十元正

2015 年 10 月 1 日初版

25. Having spent nearly all our
A
money, we couldn't afford to
stay at a hotel.

(A) Having spent (B) To spend
(C) Spent
(D) To have spent

= As we had spent nearly all...
完成式的分詞表「比主要動詞先發生」。
stay at a hotel 住旅館
暫住 長住用 live。

26. — When shall I call, in the
D   morning or afternoon?
    — Either. I'll be in all day.

(A) Any   (B) None
(C) Neither (D) Either

either = 兩者任一
any   三者(或以上)任一

When shall I call
= When do you want me
    to call

27. He is thought to have
B
acted foolishly. Now he

has no one but himself

to blame for losing the job.

(A) to act   (B) to have acted
(C) acting   (D) having acted

28. It was the middle of the
D
night when my father woke

me up and told me to watch

the football game.

(A) that   (B) as
(C) which   (D) when

(A) → It was in the middle of
      the night that...

29. Children, when accompanied by
D
their parents, are allowed to

enter the stadium.

(A) to be accompanied
(B) to accompany
(C) accompanying
(D) accompanied

when   ⎫
while ⎬ (they are) accompanied
在   ⎪ 省略主詞和 be動詞。
as   ⎭

stadium n. 體育館
museum n. 博物館

30. If Mr. Dewey had been present,
B he would have offered any possible assistance to the people there.
    (A) were   (B) had been
    (C) should be   (D) was
    Dewey [ˈdjuɪ] n. 杜威
    與過去事實相反,用 had pp.

31. — I've prepared all kinds of food for the picnic.
D   — Do you mean we needn't bring anything with us?
    (A) can't   (B) mustn't
    (C) hasn't   (D) needn't
    needn't + V原 不需要

32. You will never gain success
D unless you are fully devoted to your work.
    (A) when   (B) because
    (C) after   (D) unless
    unless 除非 (= if…not)
    be devoted to 專心於
                  ↑

33. There is no greater pleasure
B than lying on my back in the middle of the grassland, staring at the night sky.
    (A) to stare   (B) staring
    (C) stared   (D) having stared
    分詞構句對前面的話加以補充說明。

lie on one's back 平身尚
lie on one's stomach 足小基
lie on one's side 側小尚
grassland 草地

34. Since the time humankind
B started gardening, we have been trying to make our environment more beautiful.
    (A) try   (B) have been trying
    (C) are trying   (D) will try

humankind 人類
= mankind
= human beings
garden v. 從事園藝
since + 過去式, 主要子句用完成式。
現在完成進行式 > 現在完成式

35. __Make__ what you're doing
A
today important, because
you're trading a day of
your life for it.

(A) Make   (B) To make
(C) Making (D) Made

trade ... for ~ 以...交換~

要重視你今天所做的事

36. It's __not__ doing the things we
A
like, but liking the things
we have to do __that__ makes
life happy.

(A) that   (B) how
(C) what   (D) who

not A but B 不是A而是B

It is + 強調部分 + that + 其餘部分

去掉 It is 和 that，恢復原句。

37. __To free__ ourselves from
C
physical and mental tensions
身   心   緊張
we each need deep thought
                        深思
and inner peace.
內心的 平靜
(A) Having freed   (B) Freed
(C) To free   (D) Freeing

To free = In order to free
free A from B 使A免於B

38. I've been trying to phone
A
Charles all evening, but there
must be something wrong with
the network; I can't seem
to __get through__.

(A) get through 接通(電話)
(B) get off 下(車)
(C) get in 上(車)
(D) get along 進展

39. Is this your necklace, Mary?
A
I __came across__ it when I was
cleaning the bathroom this
morning.

(A) came across (偶然發現; 偶然
遇到) (= find ... by chance)
(B) dealt with 處理
(C) looked after 照顧
(D) went for 試

40. Check carrots, potatoes, onions
B
and any other vegetables in
storage, and immediately
use or throw away any which
show signs of rotting.
腐爛的跡象
(A) In demand 需求量大
(B) in storage 儲存的
(C) on loan 租借的
(D) on sale 廉價出售

41. [Once you start eating in
D   a healthier way,] weight
    control will become much
    easier.

    (A) Unless   (B) Although
    (C) Before   (D) Once ─一旦

42. In addition to the school, the
B   village has a clinic, which

43. [Clearly and thoughtfully
C   written,] the book inspires
    confidence in students who
    wish to seek their own
    answers.

    (A) writing   (B) to write
    (C) written   (D) being written
    = (As it is) clearly and thoughtfully
    written, …

最是一種語言，是由數個不同的文化
群佳共同使用，每一個群佳使用的
方式都不同。
diverse [daɪ'vɝs] adj 不同的
    (= different)
Chinglish = Chinese-English
    How long you stay in Taiwan?
→ How long have you lived
    in Taiwan?

was also built with government
support.

(A) In reply to   (B) In addition to
(C) In charge of   (D) In place of

{ in addition to 除了…之外
| = besides   (還有)
{ = other than
| = apart from
{ = aside from

with government support
= with money given by the
  government
clinic n. 診所 (= a small hospital)

因為這本書寫得很清楚，考慮周到，它
激發了學生的信心，想要自己尋找答案。

44. English is a language shared
B   by several diverse cultures,
    each of which uses it
    differently.

    (A) all of which   (B) each of which
    (C) all of them   (D) each of them

45. The two countries will
D   meet to break down
    trade barriers.
       貿易   障礙
    (A) make up 組成
    (B) use up 用完
    (C) turn down 拒絕
    (D) break down 清除；打破